Shelter from the Storm
An Anthology

Black Beacon Books

Shelter from the Storm
Published by Black Beacon Books
Edited by Cameron Trost
Cover photography and design by Cameron Trost.
Photograph taken in Saint-Nazaire, France, during the storm of the 26th of December, 2017.
Copyright © Black Beacon Books, 2018

Absinthe for the Soul © Danielle Birch
Deep-Sea Fishing © Claire Fitzpatrick
The Murder at Karreg Du © Cameron Trost
The Bells of St. Clement's © Stuart Olver
Creep's Motel © Jeremy Hayes
And Then There Were Two © Pym Schaare
The Inimitable Livers © Mark McAuliffe

Black Beacon Books
blackbeaconbooks.com

ISBN: 978-0-9923211-2-3

This anthology is dedicated to all who love stormy weather, whether it be the thunderstorms of the tropics, the tempests of the Atlantic, or the blizzards of the frozen north. Seek shelter, batten down the hatches, and lose yourself in this short anthology of suspense, mystery, and terror, designed to be read in one stormy sitting while the wind howls or thunder bellows.

Want more thrilling anthologies from Black Beacon Books?

The Black Beacon Books of Mystery
The Black Beacon Book of Ghosts
The Black Beacon Book of Horror
The Black Beacon Book of Pirates
Steampunk Sleuths
Tales from the Ruins
A Hint of Hitchcock
Murder and Machinery
Lighthouses
Subtropical Suspense

How about a novel or a collection?

Flicker by Cameron Trost
Dark Reflections by Paul Kane
Fortitude by Karen Bayly

www.blackbeaconbooks.com

The Stormy Stories

Author Biographies

Absinthe for the Soul
Danielle Birch

1928
Summer

Lorcan

It began with a smattering of rain that quickly turned into a downpour. It smothered all other sound, fogged the windows and made the house steamy and unbearable. Every day this week, almost as soon as the sun farewelled another sweltering day, the deluge began.

Lightning filled the sky and thunder boomed as hell unleashed upon us. In the dining room, my boarders played cards under flickering lights. It was a regular Friday night thing but tonight I couldn't bring myself to join. I hadn't produced a single word at the typewriter today, yesterday, last week. Unlike them, writers and poets who flaunted their achievements. Their elation and congratulatory toasts about their own wordage was almost my undoing. Abandoned at my desk, salvaged scraps of notes were a jumbled mess of words. I had no idea how to mould them into anything resembling the poetry I'd once committed to paper. I was reminded again of all that had been lost and how bitterly I fought to survive it.

I lit a cigarette and shook the match free of its flame, watched as they drank, smoked, flipped cards. Outside, another flash of lightning was followed by thunder.

Ray set his cards down face up and grinned, baring crooked teeth. The others groaned and tossed their cards in. The lights flickered again. I butted my cigarette and went hunting for candles.

I was fossicking in the hall cupboard when I heard knocking. At first, I thought it was a tree branch hitting the side of the house, then realised someone was at the door.

A clap of thunder, like a cannon, and the house was plunged into darkness. I closed my hand over the box of candles and shut the cupboard. As I blindly reached for the doorknob, the lights came on. I pulled the front door open, the force of the wind slamming it into me.

A young woman stood on the threshold, drenched to her skin, long blonde hair plastered to her head. Behind her, Mother Nature raged, her mood fouler than ever.

The beautiful urchin smiled and I was transfixed, unable and unwilling to look away. Those lips. Candy apple red. Lush. Ripe. A memory washed up from the dark recesses of my mind, vivid and enticing.

I stood aside to allow her entry. I caught a whiff of her sweet scent and wrestled with the door as she dripped water onto the hall runner. When it was closed and the weather was banished, I turned back to her.

Otherworldly, ethereal, bedraggled. She clutched a little suitcase and appealed to me with doe eyes. Silver bracelets on her wrists jangled as she flicked her hair off her shoulders, like a cat with a bell.

'Please tell me you have a room for rent,' she said, glancing up the stairs to the second floor.

I didn't have the heart to tell her there were no vacancies. For the first time since I'd opened my house as a writer's retreat, I regretted filling the rooms upstairs. Yet I couldn't eject her back into the storm. It wasn't just the innocence or vulnerability of a young woman travelling on her own. Nor was it the fact that she wore no shoes. It was that she struck something primal deep inside me, something I thought I'd lost a long time ago. And with it, the urge to write again burned right to the tips of my fingers.

I led her to the back of the house, to my own private rooms.

Her clothes needed to be stripped off and she'd need towels, maybe a bath.

I closed my eyes, desire stirring deep in my loins.

One of the boarders put on a record and Mamie Smith started singing about the crazy blues. I exchanged the candles for a towel and handed it to her before showing her to the tiny bedroom beside mine. It had a large, north-facing window that overlooked the garden, and though it was sparsely furnished, it was comfortable.

'This is all I can offer. Bed's not made up but I'll get you some sheets,' I said as I contemplated the thinness of the walls, of having her so near. 'Bathroom's the next door down. Feel free to run a bath. Come through to the kitchen when you're done and I'll make you something to eat. I'm Lorcan, by the way.' I lit a cigarette and turned around.

She was staring out the window, into the night.

Evangeline

I stood in the centre of the room, suitcase at my feet. Lorcan had left the room abruptly, hadn't even asked my name. Was it sweet of him to take me in without asking who I was or where I'd come from? Or was it something else? I'd recognised mild desperation in his eyes when he spoke, with a faint trace of an Irish accent, sensed him wanting to reach out and touch me. Part of me had wanted him to, just so I could feel human contact again.

The rain eased as quickly as it had started and I heard laughter in other rooms, smelled damp and mustiness and cigarette smoke. I went to the door and peered into the hall. There was a general shabbiness to the mismatched furniture and threadbare rugs. Even the paintings on the walls looked faded, portraits of people who frowned or bowls of fruit that looked rotten. A malaise shrouded everything, making me feel like the lights should be kept on day and night.

9

I turned back to the room. The hardwood floors were stained dark and the walls papered with faded roses. The chenille bedspread was a washed out violet and the lampshade's torn fringing dangled drunkenly. Hanging above the narrow bed was a portrait of a woman kneeling beside a lake, hair in a long plait and lips stained the darkest red.

I turned away from it.

I refused to cry.

Not here.

A rumble of thunder made me jump and I wondered how much longer the storm would rage, and where it was headed. All those hours in the dark, losing my way, rain hammering me until I thought it might send me mad.

And now I was here, taken in by a stranger.

Lorcan had a kind face, though somewhat weathered and crinkly. There was something almost fatherly about him in the way he seemed to want to make sure I was okay. I liked that he didn't ask questions or seem curious about where I'd come from or why I'd arrived so abruptly.

I had a quick wash in the bathroom, mindful that there was no lock on the door. The clothes inside my suitcase felt damp and I pulled on my best dress—a sunset orange day dress—and dried my hair as best I could before turning to the mirror to inspect myself. The image betrayed my uncertainty and I pulled a face.

Lorcan

When I looked up, she was standing in the doorway. She'd dried her hair and changed her clothes, the silk of her dress falling seductively over her lithe frame. She'd removed the bracelets but her feet were still bare.

The others continued with their card game, oblivious to her presence, and I watched her watching them. I hadn't forewarned them of this sudden, mysterious guest, and the longer I left it, the longer she was just mine.

Suddenly, I was a mass of nerves. I wanted to sweep her away, back to the bedroom at the rear of the house so they'd never know she was here. What did it matter to them? They wrote all day, while I couldn't so much as muster the strength to touch a single key of my typewriter. It sat in the middle of my desk, mocking me, calling me a sad fucking coward.

The storm intensified again and rain pummelled the windows, rattling the glass. I gave the darkness a second's glance before returning my attention to her. What was it about this enchanting waif?

I rubbed at my arms as a shiver racked my frame. I didn't know what the others would make of her. This group of writerly sorts had grown close, gathering around the table each evening to eat and drink, argue over pages of works in progress, the house buffering them from the world outside.

One by one they looked up, cards forgotten in their appraisal of her. She seemed not to mind the visual interrogation and there was something almost belligerent about her expression as though she expected them to want to look at her. They ate her up, from her flawless skin and tea coloured eyes, to her small but pert breasts that took me back to a youth I sorely missed.

Ray's cigarette burned down to his fingers and he butted it into an overflowing ashtray before leaping to his feet.

'What's your name, sweetie,' he said, bending to lower himself to her level.

'Evangeline,' she answered in a polite, virginal tone.

Evangeline.

Like honey on the tongue.

I held my breath, rejoiced in her existence. It was as though an angel had flown into the room.

A crack of thunder made her jump. Ray winked and slid an arm around her slender shoulders. 'Don't you worry, pet. It'll blow over soon.'

He shot me a snake-like grin as he gave her his seat. I fumed as he handed her a drink, witnessed the smile she bestowed on him that should have been mine.

Ray was the longest boarder I'd had, more a resident now that he'd been here over a year. When he wasn't drinking, he ghosted the house, likely never to finish what he was working on because he kept changing his protagonist's motivation.

To my left, Xavier cleared his throat and moved his chair closer to Evangeline. 'My dear, you're a breath of delight, bursting in on this stormy eve.'

I was irritated by the way he spoke, almost as though he'd leaped from the pages of a Victorian novel. He took off his glasses and leaned in, like he was viewing an exhibit at a fair. He was a poet, and an ordinary one at that. His desire for melodrama caused him to produce an extraordinary amount of mentally challenging prose that none of us had much of a stomach for. I could picture him forming his next verse in Evangeline's honour, imagined his overblown use of verbs. He was supposed to be leaving tomorrow, but I suspected that come morning he'd be at the table, reciting his latest work, hoping for an adoring audience in Evangeline.

'Wine, Lorcan?'

I turned. Ray was holding a bottle of claret. He glanced briefly at Evangeline before raising an eyebrow in my direction.

'Have you gifted us a muse?' he said.

I sneered at him as I retrieved my glass. My nerves jangled at the thought of this waif sleeping with just a thin wall separating us.

Ray filled the glass to the brim, smirking at me as though he could read my mind. Smug bastard.

In the corner, Vivien watched Evangeline, cigarette smoke curling around an unforgiving grimace. She cleared her throat and opened her arms like a queen addressing her minions. 'How lucky we are that you found us,' she said. 'This isn't a night for travelling.'

Outside, wind howled as the storm deepened into a tyrant of fury. The lights went out briefly, and when they came back on, Evangeline was pale. Vivien smiled at her like a feline about to pounce.

Vivien was a poet, like Xavier, but she had a talent for words that he could only hope to aspire to. She spoke of little but Emily Dickinson and the frequent nightmares she suffered in which she was drowned by ex-lovers.

'Are you a writer?' Vivien asked in her lazy drawl.

'Me?' Evangeline looked disconcerted. 'No…I'm…maybe someday.'

I watched her carefully. She didn't seem particularly taken with any of them. Even delicate Jasper, standing to the side, glasses perched on the end of his nose, eyes sparkling with cunning. There was always something darker at play with Jasper. It was the way his mouth curled as though he was about to say something disparaging or commit an act of cruelty.

Evangeline

Their attention was overwhelming. They refilled my glass and Lorcan brought me a plate of egg and pickle sandwiches. I took tiny bites and studied the room, which was teeming with books and maps. It was a big room, though it appeared smaller because of the noise they made and the oversized furniture that was badly in need of a polish. The walls were papered in a burgundy damask, clashing with brown striped curtains. The paintings were all landscapes. It resembled a home that had been loved once and now was merely a house.

I finished the sandwiches and sipped the wine, silently amused by the way they watched me. As they flipped cards and accused each other of cheating, I noticed how Ray treated the others with mild disdain. He was older, his faced deeply lined, as opposed to Lorcan's rugged handsomeness and Xavier and Jasper's unmarked youth. I wasn't sure about Vivien, though

13

her cynicism and aloofness made her seem older.

Ray slammed his cards down on the table and I jumped, spilling my wine.

'You cheating cur,' he growled at Xavier. 'What do you think you're doing?'

'Nothing.' Xavier's voice dripped with innocence.

Ray shot to his feet, leaned across the table and grabbed Xavier by the throat. 'Admit you cheated.'

'I did not.'

I didn't see who head-butted whom, only that they stumbled backwards rubbing their heads. It spiralled quickly and I leaped from my chair as punches were thrown. Lorcan swore, threw a glass that hit Ray squarely on the nose. Fists flew and insults were hurled back and forth.

'Nothing to do with cheating,' Xavier said. 'Why don't you say what it's really about?'

'You shut your mouth,' Ray said.

'Let's not get all worked up,' Jasper said as Ray swung a punch at Xavier.

I closed my eyes as Vivien told them all not to be so fucking melodramatic. It was the first time I'd heard someone say *fuck*. I opened my eyes and stared as they stopped fighting for the briefest of moments, before Ray snarled something at Xavier and they began all over.

Nerves shredded by the tempest outside and the actions of these crazy people, I excused myself and sought the solitude of my room.

When I was curled up in bed, I wished for the sky to stop spitting vitriol. The storm rampaged with no hint of surrender and the crack of thunder rattled my teeth. I stared through the pale, threadbare curtains as the lightning made it seem, just for a second or two, as if it was morning.

Then suddenly it was all over. The rain stopped and in the welcoming silence I opened a window to let the breeze in. I was about to return to bed when I heard a scraping noise.

14

Putting it down to the quirks of an unfamiliar house, I climbed into bed. Floorboards creaked above, followed by something heavy being dragged across the floor. I rolled onto my back, thought I heard tapping at my door.

Sitting up, I waited for it again, but there was only the arthritic groan of the refrigerator in the kitchen. I imagined Lorcan in the next room, alone in his bed. Was he unable to sleep?

Every time I'd caught him looking at me, eyes watered with pleading, I wasn't sure if it was because he ached to touch me or whether I reminded him of someone else.

Lorcan

When the first rays of daylight cleaved through the trees, I was at the typewriter. Evangeline's appearance had breathed new life into me and my fingers burned as they flew over the keys. My creative drought was over.

Evangeline.

My saviour. My undying joy.

The very thought of her ignited a spark and chased the bleakness from my soul. Her smile warmed my blood. I needed this. I needed her. Everything about her. Alabaster skin, slender frame. And her voice. Her laugh. It was a melody. A choir. A fucking symphony. I'd been awakened. Enlightened. Willingly enslaved by the body and mind of an angel. I would love her like no one else. I would give her everything.

Her spirit spilled onto the paper in fluid prose. It made sense. My jumbled notes made sense. Evangeline made it real. She was more alive than anyone I'd known.

Evangeline

Another storm blew up that evening as I hovered by Lorcan's bedroom door, calmed by the clattering of the typewriter. He'd been in there most of the day, lost in his own world while I explored the house, managing to avoid the others. I ached to be outside, to cross the road and walk the seawall and breathe the fresh air, but I didn't want to leave the house.

When Lorcan tensed I knew he'd realised someone was behind him.

'Keep typing,' I said.

It took him a moment to compose himself. He trembled the way a drunk does when desperate for another drop. I entered the room and fingered some of the things on his desk. Shark teeth. A possum tail. Copper coins in a brass bowl. A small, egg-shaped portrait of a pale blonde woman. Young. Vulnerable. Unclouded and unruffled. I didn't run my fingers over it as I had the other items, but stared at her as though she might tell me something more about Lorcan.

He returned to his typing and I leaned forward and whispered, 'How long until dinner?'

'It might be a little late. I've started something new.' He tore a sheet of paper from the typewriter and shoved it into a drawer.

'I'll find one of the others,' I said with a faint smile as the rumbling outside continued.

I was at the door when he whispered, 'Don't ever leave, Evangeline.'

Lorcan

I wanted Evangeline at my side. I didn't want the others feeding off her youth. Already they circled, preying on her with their questions, watching her talk, eat, move. They were taking everything they could from her, and I needed it so much more than them.

I'd managed to write more in one day than I had all year. All because of her. I'd thought of nothing but her as my fingers danced over the keys. The verses flowed, sweetness and light,

16

torment and folly. In this new story, a monster hunted my muse, forcing her to perform outrageous acts of treachery and perversion. A tragedy forced her to flee, delivering her into her hero's arms.

When it was finished and Evangeline had read it, she'd understand what she meant to me. Then she'd truly be mine.

Triumphant, I pulled another page from the typewriter. It had been done before; an older man in love with a much younger woman. But when the woman was in danger, when degenerates preyed on her for their own filthy needs, she needed to be protected. And I had a fresh angle.

I had Evangeline.

Evangeline

Xavier approached me first.

He invited me up to his room after dinner. Inspiration for his latest work, he said. A series of poems about a woman lost. I told him I wasn't lost. He asked me to pose nude so he could capture the female form at her most vulnerable and write in the most honest way he knew. Meeting his eyes, I asked him why nudity should make a woman vulnerable. He shrugged, mumbled something about it being the eternal question.

Curious to learn more about his writings, I shed my clothes and he asked me to stand by the window.

'No one can ever really know where they're going,' he said. 'You think you have control of your destiny but you can't know beyond this moment.' He leaned forward.

He was so close I could feel his breath hot on my skin. I wanted to stand back but something compelled me to stay where I was, goose bumps peppering my flesh.

'Let me read something of yours,' I said, fixated on the red typewriter in the middle of his bed.

When I saw the look in his eyes, I knew there was nothing he'd refuse me. 'Maybe after I've sketched you.'

I watched him watching me. Nimble fingers on paper, hurried, as though he was afraid I'd vanish.

When he'd finished, I dressed and took his chapters, the paper crinkling like they'd been screwed up and tossed out before being retrieved from the rubbish.

In my room, with the door firmly closed, I devoured every word. It flowed beautifully, like the foxtrots I remembered my grandparents doing. Each verse swept me up in a fantasy, gripping me, entertaining me and horrifying me so much that I laughed until finally I wept.

Xavier found me and handed me a handkerchief. He waited while I blew my nose and then I told him it was the most wonderful thing I'd ever read. I asked him how long it had taken him to write and he spluttered something about it coming to him one night in a moment of despair.

And then, as our eyes met, I saw the naked desire in his.

I handed him the pages and fled.

Lorcan

Evangeline, sun in my heart, food for my blood.

Every word on the paper, all of it, because of her.

Nourishment for my soul. Food for my ever-starving mind.

I wanted to ask her to sit with me so I could look at her while I worked, as if she were posing for a painting, though I'd be committing her to fiction. Deflowering her with my words.

While searching for her, I overheard her in the front room with Jasper, and listened at the door.

'Tell me what you think?' Jasper said. 'Tell me this is the most beautiful thing you've ever read.'

There was a short silence broken by the rustling of paper.

'It's magical,' Evangeline said. 'Though you make it seem as though living is futile. You convince me when I don't want to be convinced.'

'Your interpretation is exquisite,' he said, and I fumed in the hall, wondered what it was she'd read. I wanted to grab Jasper's scrawny throat and squeeze every breath from him.

'Let me see more,' she said, and I sensed urgency in her tone.

'Maybe you should come to my room later. There's less chance of being overheard. You never know who's lurking down here,' he said, and I wondered if they'd somehow guessed I was listening in. 'I'd be careful about getting around at night too. There's supposed to be a ghost.'

I heard her indrawn breath, imagined her hand at her throat, her lips lightly parted.

'Tell me about the ghost,' she said.

'There isn't much to say, though a previous guest was so traumatised we think it might have caused his death. It happened not long ago, late at night. In full disclosure, he'd been drinking and he fell down the stairs and broke his neck. I shared a room with him. Nice chap.'

I didn't hear what Evangeline said, only the tinkle of glasses. She was drinking with him, in the afternoon, and I imagined her sweet rosy lips pressed to the rim of the glass.

Christ, I wanted her. To caress her skin and run my tongue the length of her body. I wanted to be witness to every movement she made, every word she uttered, everything her soft lips touched.

Evangeline

Lorcan placed violets in my room. He used a milk glass for a vase and some of the flowers drooped, victims of the heat, but it was the thought. I guess. Part of me liked it. It was a dangerous way to think, but I allowed myself a few seconds to feel flattered that he'd wanted to do something nice for me.

I crept through the house, keen to remain invisible. No one was about and I hurried up the stairs, stole into Ray's room and scanned the mess. Unmade bed. Empty whiskey bottles.

19

Clothes hanging over the backs of chairs. His typewriter was balanced on a pile of books, a large dent in the side. Next to it, a manuscript. I hadn't wanted to ask to see his work, couldn't bear the thought of being alone with him, and I'd seized the moment when I heard him telling Vivien he was going out for cigarettes. Confident I'd hear anyone coming, I crossed the room and lifted the first page.

Eyes wide, I drowned in the rich text of lust, romance, and impending doom. A gateway to another world where love was fictional, sex was traded like currency, and there was no fear of hope.

A door slammed somewhere in the house and I jumped, dropped the papers onto the desk. I'd lost track of time. I flew down the stairs, my heart thundering. I passed Ray in the gloomy hall, barely giving him a glance as my face flamed.

There was no sound from Lorcan's room and I paused outside the door. No clack of the typewriter. I swallowed, hands at my side, and nudged the door open with my toe.

He was sitting on the side of his bed. His hair was askew, his eyes wild, and my instinct was to turn and run.

'Why are you here?' he said as he looked up.

'The storm,' I answered, my heart still racing. He looked as though he was angry with me.

'It only lasted a few hours.' He sounded doubtful. 'What was your intended destination that night?'

I stared at him, level-eyed. 'I had no destination. Only an escape.'

His eyes widened. 'Is someone looking for you?'

'No,' I said. 'I'm alone.'

He smiled slowly, and the anger dissolved. 'You're not alone, my dear. You'll never be alone here. Why don't you come in and sit down?'

Stepping into the room, I hesitated before sitting on the corner of the bed. He smiled again, eyes filled with watery desperation.

'Will you let me see something you've written?' I asked, knees slightly parted. He wanted to look down, I knew he did, but he maintained eye contact.

'I'll show you something I've written if you promise not to spend too much time with the others.'

'Why?'

'They're untrustworthy. Swine, all of them. Not the sort of people you should be associating with.'

'Why have them here?'

'This is a writer's retreat. They're writers. Their money keeps this place going.'

I considered his words, watched his fingers shake as he lit a cigarette. 'What do you know about the ghost?' I asked.

A flicker of uncertainty, then he looked down and was silent for so long I didn't think he was going to answer. I was about to repeat the question when he turned to me, eyes haunted.

'There is no ghost,' he said, his face pale.

'But everyone...'

'It's a tale fabricated by one of my boarders for his own amusement,' he said.

'Which one?'

He paused for the longest time. 'He isn't here now. He was...he's gone.'

Lorcan

It was late afternoon when I looked up as Evangeline passed my room. My barefoot bohemian had washed her hair and it shone as it hung down her back. I tried not to imagine her lying in the tub, wet hair clinging to her, firm little breasts rising out of the water.

I went to the door, smelled her freshness on the air, and followed her down the hall.

She climbed the stairs, bare feet silent on the carpet.

Vivien appeared in the hall, reached out a gentle hand and

pulled Evangeline into her room.

My feet hardly touched the stairs, and I ducked into the bathroom that shared a wall with Vivien's room. As I closed the door and flicked the lock, I spied a glass on the vanity. I snatched it up, pressed it to the wall and listened.

'Such exquisite eyes.' Vivien's voice, masterful. She was like a filthy alley cat, purring over her prey. 'You remind me of someone I once knew.'

'Really,' Evangeline said. 'Tell me about her.'

'But I'd rather talk about you. Cigarette?'

'Yes, please.'

Silence followed, and I imagined Vivien sliding a cigarette between Evangeline's soft red lips, lighting it, and then Evangeline inhaling before she released the smoke in a haze. How I wanted to keep her in my room, never let her see anyone but me. She was life. An elixir. I was barely able to keep up with the ideas flooding my head, could barely type fast enough to expel them onto paper.

'Tell me about the ghost,' Evangeline said, and I imagined Vivien observing her as she smoked her cigarette.

'It's something to be seen, not talked about, apparently.'

'I asked the others, but they've been so vague.'

Vivien let out a cynical chuckle. 'Don't imagine you'll get too much out of the men in this house. They're only here to take, not to give. Remember that.'

There was a short silence and then I heard a chair being dragged across the floor, followed by muffled laughter.

'Let me read something of yours,' Evangeline said.

'Help yourself, kiddo. There's a stack of pages next to my bed.'

Rustling paper, words whispered, followed by the melodious sound of a woman's laughter. It drove me wild, and I wanted to beat down the door and rescue Evangeline from Vivien's clutches.

Finally, the clacking of keys, and soon after, Evangeline's

words, 'This is…what you wrote…it breaks my heart. It's so real. It's the absolute truth about everything.'

Evangeline

It was Jasper who suggested we have a drink to celebrate my arrival. He called me a shot of glorious sunshine in tumultuous weather.

I didn't miss the venom in Lorcan's eyes or the bemusement in Vivien's. They watched each other nearly as much as they watched me, like they were each waiting for the other to swoop.

Yet another storm was on the cusp when Jasper broke from the card game and went for the whiskey bottle. My nerves were shredded by the savagery of the storms and their nightly appearance, as though they were trying to destroy the house and everything inside.

Jasper was unscrewing the bottle when I spied the absinthe in the corner and leaped up, nearly knocking over a bedraggled fern.

'Let me,' I said, feeling the weight of their gazes as I brandished the absinthe bottle.

They looked from the bottle to me and back again. I didn't think I was mistaken when I saw discomfort in their expressions.

In the corner cupboard, I found little red glasses, took them into the kitchen and filled them before adding a little something extra. Outside, a flash of white across the darkening sky was followed by a deep, low rumble.

When I carried the tray in, they barely looked up from their game. I placed a drink before each of them, and it wasn't until I sat down and they reached for the glasses that I realised they hadn't been concentrating on the game at all.

'You're not having one?' Ray said.

'I don't have much of a head for alcohol,' I said.

'Nonsense, pet.' Ray leaped up and dug out another glass. 'You're never too young to prepare your liver for the art of drinking.'

Lorcan threw his shot back and sucked in a sharp breath. I knew that feeling. Fast, blinding heat. Liquid rage.

I drank the shot.

The liquid was scathing as it navigated my throat and I coughed, covered my mouth with my hand.

Ray smiled, teeth bared like a crocodile as I collected empty glasses and took them back to the kitchen to refill. Mother Nature was unleashing her worst and I'd only just finished filling the last glass before the power died.

Another crack of thunder.

When would it end?

A soft breath on my neck.

I froze.

'I have a candle.' A deep voice. So close.

The strike of a match and then the soft glow. Lorcan's face inches from mine.

'Don't be afraid, child,' he said. 'Let me help you.'

Before I could speak, he set the candle down on the tray and carried it through to the dining room. I followed, took his seat when he insisted, and watched as he lit more candles.

He returned to his seat, handed a glass to me, and I felt them watching, waiting, like tigers ready to pounce.

'I hope I see the ghost tonight,' I said, despite Lorcan's earlier words, saw fear in the men's eyes and scorn in Vivien's.

'There is no ghost,' Ray said. 'Only the idea of one.'

'What do you mean?'

'Sometimes we think we see something.' Ray's expression was grim. 'We drink too much, and then we fantasise, seek out what isn't really here.'

He was lying.

Ray threw back his shot. They all did. Suddenly they seemed eager for the oblivion that only something like absinthe could bring.

I had to be careful. I needed my wits. No nerves.

Not now.

They had no idea.

Lorcan

I hadn't seen the bottle of absinthe since the night Gabriel died. We'd all indulged, and then, after we'd gone to bed, the ruckus. I'd ignored it. Later, there'd been a storm and the power hadn't come back on until morning. By then, Gabriel was dead at the foot of the stairs. The absinthe bottle had been returned to the liquor cabinet and no one had touched it since.

Until now.

None of us had talked about what had happened that night, and I still didn't want to think about it. I looked at Evangeline, thought of the way her neck arched when she'd taken that first shot. Her pale throat, skin young and supine.

Anything that sweet and innocent couldn't be bad for you.

Just one shot.

I said it every time. But then there was an itch for a second. More of the delicious nectar to blemish reality.

One more.

Like honey from the mouths of goddesses.

Radiance.

Evangeline filled the glasses again. A third. Or was it the fourth? The forbidden fourth. The shot that might tip you over the edge as you began to lose count. Sometimes after the fourth, it's difficult to distinguish what's real. I didn't need any more but I'd have it anyway.

Warmth. Sunny delight. Rays of gleaming hope.

Tonight, the answer was in front of me, as it had been since the minute she'd entered my house.

Evangeline.

She was a drug. I was feverish, dying for her. Last night I'd

25

watched her sleep, stood over her, the steady rise of her bare chest. It had been too much. I was weak. Fallible. Human. I'd reached out, softly caressed her nipple, hard like a pebble. I would happily burn in hell for this angel, delivered to me.

I needed to protect her from the wolves.

Evangeline

Each time they threw their heads back and drank the shots, I poured mine into the fern. They didn't suspect a thing.

Colourless. Odourless. Tasteless.

They held out their glasses for more and I took them to the kitchen, refilled them purposefully and without remorse.

They remained clueless. They were celebrating. They'd had a productive week and they were slapping each other on the back.

By candlelight, I watched as they became drunker and more uncertain, started to slur and stumble. The poison took hold in Lorcan first. His face grew redder and redder until he excused himself, mumbled something about his stomach. They lost focus, forgot words, spat accusations, and Xavier's bowels expelled from him.

They went to bed, all of them so ill, and soon the house was quiet. I tidied up, rinsed glasses and returned the absinthe to the cabinet.

I was sure now that Gabriel's writings had never left this house. In all of their pages, wielded proudly as though it was their own work, I'd recognised the words of my love. He'd been writing about me. His muse. His inspiration. When he was finished, he was coming for me. We were to be married and begin our life together. Except, he never left this house alive.

Because of what they did to him.

It was one of them. It was all of them.

As I lay in bed, the storm thrashing the very life out of the house, I imagined them writhing in their beds. When I could no

26

longer stand the anticipation, I crept from my room and pressed my ear to Lorcan's door. He was moaning, shrieking gibberish, begging for mercy.

I went back to my room.

Waited.

Later, when the storm had been swept out to sea, I heard their mutterings.

Lorcan

I tried to scream out for Evangeline. Tried to crawl across the floor. Every time I moved, I was gripped by a vile pain. It burned my stomach, tore through my soul.

Evangeline, why can't you hear me?

And my eyes. They blurred and watered until I could no longer see. Dizziness and nausea struck over and over, my gut heaving like a boat tossed about in a storm.

Evangeline, please hear me.

It had to be something I ate.

More likely something I'd drunk.

It had to be one of them. Or all of them. None could be trusted. What had I been thinking, letting them live here?

Dirty vultures. Feeding off me.

And Evangeline.

My darling Evangeline.

Without me, she'd be at their mercy.

Evangeline, oh my Evangeline, why don't you hear me?

Evangeline

I listened to their anguish all through the night as the poison hooked its claws in. They howled and brayed, screaming for help. Lorcan's agony was the loudest, but perhaps it was because he was in the next room. I imagined him curled into a ball, clutching his chest, eyes bulging as the poison claimed him.

At one stage, their screams grew so loud I covered my ears. I shook, and wept, and thought of my beautiful Gabriel, used and abandoned by people he'd thought of as friends.

Every day he'd lived here, he'd written me a letter. Sometimes, it was no more than a poem, but every word was precious. He'd been happy here. His novel was coming along and he was close to finishing. And then he'd died. His body had been taken from this house and no one had been able to say what had happened. His parents had buried him and these people had gone on living.

People who'd stolen from him.

People who were responsible for his death.

I was still awake at dawn, but there was finally silence. From room to room, I checked on them. None were breathing. Lorcan was hunched over his desk and Jasper looked as though he'd tried to make it to the door. I pictured him staggering, reaching for the handle, before collapsing. Xavier looked like he was trying to embrace someone, his eyes open but unseeing, and Ray was in the bathroom, face down in the tub.

Vivien was the worst. She'd torn at her own skin, raking it from her face as though she'd tried to shed it. As though that would save her.

I hadn't left the house since I'd arrived. No one knew I was here. No one had seen me arrive and no one would see me leave. I had Gabriel's writings, recovered from each of them. My writings now. All of it packed into my suitcase.

I tiptoed down the hall, stopped for a minute to breathe in the lingering scent of fading violets. Then I let myself out of the house.

Deep-Sea Fishing
Claire Fitzpatrick

The rain was torrential, scudding against the sloped roof of the boat. I stowed my belongings under the deck, shakily signing my name on the boat's manifest. Thomas handed me a piece of paper with my bag number.

'All right there, son?' dad called from on board. 'Get in, get in, away from the storm.'

I nodded, looking up at the wraithlike shadows accumulating in the sky. 'I'm good.'

'Did you catch the safety equipment talk?'

'Yep.'

Dad nodded. 'Don't mind the weather. A storm never frightens the fish away.'

Pete spoke over the intercom, explaining about the safety equipment, how to rig up, and giving a run-down of the night ahead. Dad told me there was an allure to deep-sea fishing which had nothing to do with the fabricated excitement of TV shows. 'It's more relaxing than you think, he said. 'We don't wrestle with giants. We think about them.'

It took thirty minutes to get out into the fishing grounds, the rain bucketing for most of the duration. Pete set up the rental gear and passed out raincoats, giving us all a quick 101. While most of the guys stuck to their beers, I kept my ears open, eyes sharp.

'Be careful you don't fall in,' said dad.

'Don't want to be sleeping with the fishes,' Aaron joked. He pulled the binoculars away from his watery blue eyes. He appeared more interested in birds than humans, and noted the different types he spotted in his notebook. Before we'd left that afternoon, Aaron had said we'd cross paths with bird migrations unperturbed by the storm, swooping around the pitch-black curtains draped across the sky, like warped, twisted shapes ducking in and out. But the creatures above were lost and confused, with some seeming to drop right out of the sky altogether, landing on the patches of driftwood floating by the boat.

'What are they doing?' I asked, hooking my bait. 'Should we tell someone? The marine people? Why are they out so late? I thought they weren't bothered by the weather.'

'The *marine people*?' dad joked.

Aaron shrugged. 'Not sure, lad. Best to leave the birds to their own devices.'

I nodded. I'd watched dad with Aaron for years. His face had carved up a perpetual expression for Aaron, one mixed with both pride and pity. I hated them both.

#

I spent the next few hours on deck, until the sun sank and we waited for midnight. Rain fell intermittently, though not hard enough for us to head below deck. I stood by the railing, line in both wet hands, staring at the mass of dark water. Time slowed as my fingers fiddled with the squid, waiting patiently for the green light. Once the boat settled, I dropped my line.

The fish came in like a pack of wild dogs, snarling, sniffing, and flailing. I pulled my shirt over my nose, trying not to breathe in the nasty odour. Dad and Aaron hauled in the first batch, opening the hatch, pulling out the tarpaulin, until the fish were tucked away under the deck.

'You gonna help me, son?' asked dad, 'I'm doing the work of two men.'

Aaron glanced at me, face impassive. I sighed, disheartened my hook had failed to catch.

'I'm going down for a sec,' I said, attaching my rod to the side of the boat. Dad waved his hand in acknowledgement.

30

Above, I could hear their laughter and their easy banter. I sighed, wishing I had the same euphoria the others felt out on the sea, though I suppose passion had more to do with endurance in the dark storm than anything else. I was certain the love of deep-sea fishing was either a learned practice, or being sick of rejection from society.

I walked down the dark, narrow hallway, peering out the little portholes at the smooth, unchanging water. Thoughts drifting, I opened the door of the room dad and I were sharing. It was small and cramped, what one might expect from a deep-sea fishing boat. Most of the confined cupboards contained fishing gear, raincoats, and endless packets of biscuits. The walls were panelled in wallpaper meant to resemble wood, and the floors were covered in rolls of crudely cut linoleum. To the left, a small enclosed shower and toilet, with a stack of toilet rolls pushed into the corner. To the right, a tall closet and corner lounge. I closed the door behind me and took off my raincoat, then climbed to the top bunk. I rolled onto my side and stared at the ornamental mirror on the wall.

'Ten thousand,' Aaron said, his shadowy form appearing in my doorway. I jumped, sitting up.

'How did you get in here? The door was locked.'

'I have my ways. It's from the Elizabethan period. It's fine craftsmanship, a collector's item. Some fishermen say it exaggerates things, reflects yourself holding a great big marlin, winning first prize. Others say it shows them something else.'

I jumped off the bed, snorting contemptuously. 'Like what? Their reflection?'

Aaron raised his eyebrows, smirking. 'You don't believe me. Your old man saw something in the mirror. Said a black smudge appeared over his left eye while he was combing his hair. Next day, fishing hook catches his eyelid, ripping it from his face.'

'Whatever. That's not how he got that scar.'

Aaron shrugged. 'Fine. Don't believe me. But you should

know Stuart was in this room before you, back when we were out for a month. He got a look at that mirror. He was your age. I told him about the mirror, your dad's fascination with it, and I assumed it'd hold some curiosity for the boy. Maybe he'd appreciate its appearance in such a dingy old boat. But he didn't.'

Crossing my arms, I traced the mirror's frame with my tired eyes. I couldn't deny the shiver of unease I felt clasp the back of my neck like the talons of an ethereal beast. 'It's an old mirror. No big deal.'

'No big deal, huh? It's sure a big deal for your dad. And it was for Stuart. Until he hanged himself.' He shrugged noncommittally. 'Your dad suggested we take you out to catch trip fish, spend a whole month together. But I said no, you wouldn't be up to spending so much time with us, with all that fish hanging on the boat for weeks. We say the fish is fresh, but can flesh stay fresh after hanging for so long? Can anything stay fresh after hanging for so long?'

Swallowing a lump of saliva, I watched as Aaron looked around the room with smug disinterest. Moonlight beaming through the porthole reflected off the mirror, leaving a pearly glow stretched across the wall behind the bunk.

'You gonna leave your line out?' Aaron said, stepping backwards. 'Your dad paid good money for you to be here, but all you're doing is hiding from the storm.'

'I'm not hiding,' I snarled, wondering how anyone could think the storm was merely rain.

Aaron rolled his eyes.

I wanted to be interested in fishing, be interested in sticking it out during the long night when the ocean grew quiet, and bankside vibrations and crisscrossing lines disappeared. I wanted to wait for the water to spring to life, as fish that refused to eat during the day let their guard down. But it all felt so menial in the storm.

'Lucian, we've got everything set up. It's piss-weak easy.

Come on. Plenty of fish and flesh in the sea. You're supposed to embrace the storm.'

I groaned, rubbing my eyes, imagining the rows of fish corpses waiting to be eaten. 'Piss off!'

Aaron narrowed his eyes. 'Come now,' he said jovially. 'I'm ya mate. Head up and see the clusters of bubbles, the disturbed silty patches, the topping fish. Use those words when you talk to your dad. He might think you care.'

'I do care! Piss off!' I repeated, moving to stand by the mirror. 'I'll be up soon.'

'If you say so. Bring your raincoat.'

Aaron winked, slinking into the darkness. Huffing, I peered into the mirror and stared at my reflection. Not for the first time, I wondered what such a thing was doing in the dingy quarters of a fishing boat. Who in their right mind would drag the mirror on board? I imagined a fish hook catching itself in my eyelid, and for a moment, it reflected in the mirror itself. I pressed my hands over my face, over my eyes, feeling for the hook. But there was nothing. Sighing, I moved to lean against the doorframe, chest heaving, fists clenched.

'Fucking arsehole.'

#

On deck, Thomas fumbled with the digital scales, patting down his pockets. Pete stood on the side of the boat, line in. He seemed fixated on the water, eyes firm, the only man somehow not drenched. Dad sat on an overturned milk crate, soft rain pouring over his face. He pulled out a small pack of batteries from his tackle box, handing them to Thomas. I watched as they worked together to get the scales operational, smiling as dad guffawed over the weight of the fish. A small, fat rat scrambled across the box, and dad jumped, dropping the fish.

'God-damned rats! C'mere, son. Hold this!'

Aaron appeared from below deck, nudging Thomas, who

then stepped in front of me to catch the fish. I ducked in front of him as dad gave me a swift pat on the back meant for Aaron. He leaped from the crate, eyes darting around for the fish. They were comfortable together, as though the only shelter they needed from the rain was each other. A crackle of thunder shot across the sky. But no one moved to go below deck, more interested in the guts of their fish and the bloodied bottles of beer in their hands.

'Leave it, mate,' Aaron said, picking his line from the side of the boat. He stood at the railing, facing the sea. Dad turned his attention to the scales.

'Horrible critters,' Pete remarked, glancing over his shoulder. I looked over at him, at his straight back, content standing on the other side of the boat in the dark, in the pounding rain, waiting for fish. He caught my eye, and I moved to stand beside him.

'Hold this,' he said, passing me the rod. I took it firmly in my hands, momentarily startled by the water's gentle hold, even in the stormy, forceful night. Pete crossed his arms, eyes scanning the darkness.

'Don't bother yourself with your dad,' he muttered. 'Thinks he knows a thing or two about everything.'

'And the mirror?'

Pete's shoulders stiffened, eyes narrowing. 'Leave it alone. You know, I looked at it once. The room moved, if only by a few centimetres. The walls turned into odd angles, balancing so precariously it seemed they would slide away into the cracks in the floorboards.'

I raised a dubious eyebrow.

'I'm serious,' Pete said. 'A dark streak of something smelling of tar blackened the side of it, across my wrist. The next day while gutting a fish, I tripped over a bucket and sliced open my arm. Your dad saved me. It was a miracle I didn't bleed to death.' He sighed, running a hand over his wet forehead. 'But you want to know what was weird? The fish

34

could smell my blood. Never had a better haul.'

Shuddering, I gripped the rod tighter, eyes narrow as I stared at the raindrops on the water. I wondered how anyone could see the fish. My hands felt unsteady, weak, and as I scanned the surface of the water for bubbles or any inclination of movement, I pondered if Pete was telling the truth. He didn't seem the type to lie. Then again, most of the men on board were reserved. There was no telling what they thought. Or planned. Still, I knew Pete believed what he was saying to be true.

After another two hours of disappointment, I realised my future would not be in the deep-sea fishing business and promptly gave up. I gazed across the cold, frothy ocean, at the low-hanging clouds, the reflection from the moon on the wavering water, imagining I was anywhere but here. Anywhere besides the middle of the ocean, with nothing but water as far as the eye could see. Dismally, I pulled in my line and stored it away. After a full eight hours of idleness and unfulfillment, I felt like a fraud. I felt dad's gaze on me as I retired once more downstairs, sodden. I dared not look back, as I knew his eyes would reflect the same disenchantment and antipathy I had for myself. I wanted to forget I was ever part of the crew. I knew dad had invited me to make use of my wasted night hours, but I returned below, dripping wet, shoulders slumped. Aaron had been right all along. I was seeking shelter. I was hiding. But not from the storm.

#

Wrapping a warm blanket around my shoulders, I sat on my bed, staring at the mirror. Rain trickled down the porthole like icy fingers trying to claw their way in. I leaned against the wall, my wet hair plastered to my forehead, wondering how the others managed to stay outside in the storm. It was already four o'clock in the morning, but the storm hadn't eased off. Don't storms usually last around half an hour? I wondered.

The moonlight cast vague shadows on the walls, each one stretching longer than the last. The smell of fish encased the room, pressing itself onto the bed, onto myself. I watched as the shadows crawled across the ornate mirror. Staring at my reflection, at the contorted angles of my cheeks, I wondered for the umpteenth time where the hell the mirror had come from. I didn't believe in ghosts, in monsters, in anything supernatural, but with mirrors...I wondered if there was more to see than my reflection.

As if detecting my curiosity, the mirror rippled. I stared at my reflection, at my sunken eyes, puffy cheeks, sallow skin, heart racing as I realised my unkempt appearance was as frightening as it was confronting. Six and a half hours on board an old fishing boat and I had somehow become a shrunken, shrivelled, sodden version of myself. But it was not a sign I was unused to seeing. Insomniacs all looked the same. I checked my bulky waterproof watch, rolling my eyes at the lateness of the hour. It would be dawn soon, and I hadn't caught a single fish.

You haven't even tried, I thought dismally. Why are you hiding? Get back out there. I stared out the window, bewildered by the continuing storm. I was no meteorologist, yet it seemed absurd the clouds had another drop left in them. Outside, the rain streaked across the glass like razors across an exposed throat. The boat rocked precariously against the gale, while waves rose as great angry mountains. The wind hurled hailstones, and the tumultuous waves spat spray over the deck.

'Hey, Lucian,' I said to myself, staring at my reflection in the mirror, 'when are you ever going to grow up?'

The reflection was silent, its mute mouth opening and closing like a suffocating fish. The skin was yellowed and tired, and the face all forehead and no cheeks. I couldn't think of any successful fisherman with a face like that.

'I don't look like them,' I muttered. 'I can never be one of them.'

'That's right.'

I jumped, tripping over myself as Aaron strode into the room, his robust presence inserting itself into every nook and cranny.

'You're such a pansy,' he said, pacing the tiny room, clothes dripping. 'Almost ten thousand, it cost.'

'You told me before.'

Aaron nodded, pressing his wet hand against his mouth. 'What are you doing here, skulking around?'

I frowned. 'It's my room. I can skulk around it if I wish. Now, go away.'

'Ah!' Aaron replied. 'But it was my room first.'

'So?'

'So, I can skulk around if I want.' He stared at me quizzically, then at the mirror, as if musing upon some great philosophical thought only he could solve. For a moment, he seemed interesting, and not the barbarous bully I knew him to be. What does my dad see in you? Why on Earth does he keep you around? You're an intimidating thug. A low-life. And I hate you.

'If you stay down here long enough looking at it, you'll go blind. Don't know why Pete bought it. It's a hideous piece of garbage.'

My thoughts became a jungle of confusion. A trickle of sweat mingled with water ran down the back of my neck.

'You said you paid ten thousand for it. Why would it be useless?'

Aaron narrowed his eyes, bemused. He ran a thick hand through his hair, sighing dramatically.

'I never said I paid for it, you snoop,' he said, moving to lean against the wall. 'I would never buy such a crappy old thing. Look at it. It's crap. A piece of junk. Why would I own it?'

I balled my hands in frustration, my heart thudding against

my chest. I took a deep breath, inhaling the stale air, and let it out, eyes fixated on Aaron.

'Was there something you wanted?'

Aaron shrugged. 'Thunderstorms, rain. Do you ever think they're supposed to wash us away?' he asked. 'Are they supposed to drench us so we become nothing but a smudge in a Monet masterpiece?'

I shrugged, body rigid, an animal ready to attack, though I was still unsure of why I was afraid of the man.

'Rain can take different forms,' Aaron continued. 'Summer thunderstorms, droplets bouncing off cars in a quick burst, torrential downpours. Yet the fish don't seem affected by it.'

He moved around the room, stopping to glance at my duffel bag, my shoes, my phone on the table beside the bunk. I bit my tongue.

'You know, fish are sensitive when it comes to the weather. They sense changes in water pressure. Insects flitter when it's sprinkling, buzzing around, enticing the fish to the surface. Rain makes humans head indoors, seek shelter with one another, but not here, out in the ocean. Not fish. When it rains, the fish come out to play. And the humans are ready.'

I ran my tongue along my bottom row of my teeth, hastily burying my hands in my pockets. A shiver ran down my back.

'What are you saying?'

Aaron shrugged, feigning disinterest. 'Oh, nothing,' he replied, moving over to the door. 'It's…' He paused, shrugging. 'Never mind.'

'What?'

'Well. There's a story about the mirror. You sure you haven't heard it?'

I shook my head irritably. 'No.'

Aaron nodded, pouting his bottom lip. 'According to the story, a fisherman once owned the mirror. Years back, hundreds of years back. He was the only survivor of a ship that sank. He got washed up on shore, somewhere on one of the

Moreton Bay islands. When the other bodies were found, it seemed there'd been an attack on the boat – knife wounds, gunshot wounds, even decapitation. You name it, those bodies had it. One man even had his eyes missing. But nobody knows who the fishermen were.'

I pulled my hands from my pockets and wrapped my arms around my waist, nodding. 'Go on.'

'Your dad told us they were taken by pirates, marauders, looking to make money. They were desperate times back then. All the land was farmhouses, cousins marrying cousins, one pub between three towns…you get the idea.'

Aaron curled his upper lip and stared through the window into the inky black night. 'Anyway, the boat washed up around the Cleveland Point Lighthouse, the original one built in 1847. You know how the second lighthouse, the one now standing, is hexagonal rather than round?'

I nodded, moving to sit on the edge of the bottom bunk. I curled my fingers under the mattress, the palms of my hands coated in sweat.

'That's because of what happened to the first one.'

'What happened to the first one?'

Aaron looked at me, eyes stern. 'The mirror.'

I breathed deeply, inhaling the stale air. Aaron moved to the window, blocking out the early morning light. A single line of sweat ran down his forehead, though he made no attempt to wipe it away. Outside, the storm battled on, hailstones thumping on the boat like marbles rattling in a box. The angry waves smacked against the side of the boat, trying to pummel their way in.

'So…the mirror?' I asked irritably, perplexed by the continuation of the seemingly unstoppable storm. I glanced at my wrist, imagining it slashed open, like Pete's fantastical story. 'I doubt a crappy old mirror could destroy a lighthouse.'

'The mirror didn't destroy the lighthouse,' Aaron replied, bemused.

39

I rolled my eyes, annoyed. 'Get your story straight, mate. You said the first one was destroyed. What? Are you going to tell me there was no lighthouse in 1847? There was no mysterious accident? Listen, I don't have time for this. My dad will be wondering where I am.'

Aaron chortled, his eyes brimming with tears. 'Your dad doesn't give a rat's arse about you. You're a failure. You know what everyone says at the pub? He's the fisherman whose son can't fish. And if you can't fish, what use are you to him? Your mum was worried. Thought you could do with paternal bonding. I heard you've been hanging out with the wrong crowd. Some old guy caught you screwing some bird at the Cleveland cemetery. You know the cemetery was moved, right?'

I shrugged. 'So?'

'They used to call it Pumpkin Point. It was swampy, and hard to keep bodies buried. Diggers couldn't dig proper graves and used poles to keep the coffins down. They built the playground over it.'

I raised my eyebrows. 'The one across from Woolworths?'

'The one and only.'

'Morbid,' I admitted. 'But what does all this have to do with the lighthouse and the mirror? It's hot in here, I'm tired, and I'm sure my dad needs you to gut fish.'

Aaron smiled. 'I'm sure *your* dad needs *you* to gut fish. If only you could be trusted with a knife.'

'I *can* be trusted with a knife,' I muttered, rubbing my tired eyes. 'I don't like fishing.'

'Child.'

Scowling, I slipped from the bunk and paced towards the mirror, staring at my reflection. Gasping, I jumped backwards, tripping over my feet. Rubbing my eyes, I peered at the mirror once more, staring at the dark reddish-brown ligature marks above my Adam's apple. Aaron raised a mocking eyebrow.

'You can see it then?'

'See what?' I snapped.

'See what's in the mirror. Or, see what's beyond the mirror.'

I turned up my nose, crossing my arm defensively. 'I saw nothing. Stop trying to scare me. You're such an arsehole, Aaron. No wonder people say you're a creep. Are you going to tell me about the lighthouse or not? I'd like to fish.'

Aaron narrowed his eyes, his expression a mix of bemusement and curiosity. Stomach knotted, I realised he liked having power over others. He liked to control and manipulate them. He'd manipulated my dad for years, and the rest of the men on the boat. Now, he was trying to manipulate me. Well, I wouldn't stand it! I had a right to be there, the same as everyone else.

'The hexagonal design and use of weatherboards are unique,' Aaron continued. 'One of the reasons you can't go inside.'

'It's closed to the public because it's old and historical.'

'No. When the mirror was there, you couldn't go inside. I mean, you physically couldn't go inside. Whoever tried to venture into the lighthouse was turned around for some reason or other, like they'd suddenly remembered to do something they'd forgotten. But when it stormed,' Aaron whispered, 'and people sought shelter in the lighthouse, whoever was granted access saw the mirror cut their throats, claiming they saw their reflection doing the very same thing. They wrote it in their suicide letters. *The mirror made me do it.* And even though the mirror is gone, is here, people say the ghosts of its victims still haunt the lighthouse. And the mirror itself.'

He raised his eyebrows, spreading his palms. 'But hey, the life of a lighthouse keeper is lonely, right? Like the life of a fisherman. Anything can happen if you peer long enough in the dark. If you seek shelter from storms, instead of embracing them. And now the mirror is here. Makes you think, huh?'

'Get out of my room.'

Aaron rolled his eyes and moved to lean against the

41

doorframe. 'You're a kid,' he said. 'You think science is bollocks and would prefer to put your faith in new-age hippy shit. But this,' he said, indicating the mirror, 'is not new-age hippy shit, and it's not something to be laughed off as a joke.'

I flipped him the bird, gesticulating wildly towards the door. 'Get out of here before I tell my dad you're harassing me.'

Aaron smirked darkly. 'You can't even catch a fish. You won't tell your dad shit. You should go to sleep.'

I slammed the door shut behind him as he slinked off down the narrow hallway, back to the deck of the boat. Inside the room, I breathed angrily, nostrils flaring, taking in the salty tang of the ocean. I could hear the voices above, but only faintly.

I wanted to be a warrior of the ocean like them. I wanted to be muscular and sturdy, my veins pumping with blood ripened by the scent of hooked and bloodied fish. I wanted to feel excitement as my fingers caressed the floppy flesh before I gutted it, warm blood running down my fingers. I wanted to be a real man, a true man, and fearlessly taste the blood in front of my peers as they eagerly cheered me on. But I was none of those things, and I knew it. The rest of the men knew it. Dad knew it. My mother, at least, clung to a semblance of hope there was still time. Maybe she was wrong?

#

Outside, the intense storm had not abated. Must be cluster storms, I thought. Dad seemed unperturbed, standing against the side of the boat, binoculars around his neck. Pete stood beside him, one foot leaning against a small blue crate, water dripping from his sodden raincoat. Two rats scurried across my feet, and I jumped backwards, bumping into John, an ancient-looking man who leaned on a cane for support. Dad liked to refer to him as my surrogate grandfather. Beside him were three plastic containers filled with fish, all dead.

42

'Hello, lad,' John said, standing aside. He tucked his long, grey beard into his belt. 'Thought you might have leaped overboard. It's five. Sun will rise in an hour or so. Where've you been?'

'I was in my room. To be honest...' I sighed, pushing my fists into my pockets. 'This isn't for me. I hate it. My dad is disappointed in me.'

John rolled his eyes. 'Your dad? Son, he likes to get under people's skin. He plays cat and mouse, but nothing else. He wants you to succeed. He wants you to do something with your life.'

I crossed my arms, huffing in irritation. 'Fucker,' I said, jerking my thumb towards Aaron. 'Told me some bullshit story about the cemetery and the creepy mirror in my room.'

'He means well, lad. Listen, I'm gonna head down for a tick. Gotta drain the main vein.' He winked. 'Will ya hold my line?'

'Sure.'

John passed his line to me and hobbled off, his cane tapping against the floorboards. I turned my gaze to the sea. It was now, dad had taught me, nautical dawn, and the sun would soon rise. I knew everyone would keep their lines in until civil dawn, when there was enough sunlight to distinguish the horizon from the sea, and the fish would swim back down to the depths of the ocean. Everyone had their lamps as the sky was still dark. Far off to the left of the sky, patches of yellow and orange poked through the darkness, like knives plunging through paper. I rubbed my tired eyes.

I felt a firm tug on John's line.

Pete raised a bushy eyebrow and said, 'I believe you've got something, Lucian.'

I held firmly to the line, glancing around for John. I glanced at Pete while wrangling John's line.

'Horrible critters,' Pete said icily, eyes steady on the horizon. 'Humans, I mean. And stupid.'

'Sorry? What?'

43

'Think they know it all. *When it rains, the fish come out to play?* Give me a break. Although, maybe I'm a fish? Not human? Bumbling idiots, they are. Everyone's an idiot. And they say fishermen are perceptive.'

His condescending tone chilled me to the bone, and I knew I had to get back to my room to see what Aaron was doing.

I glanced over at dad, silently projecting my fears. I wanted to tell him I was scared. I wanted to tell him how uncomfortable I felt. But I couldn't. He already thought I was nothing more than a snivelling, good-for-nothing child. I knew it. I watched as he bagged and tagged types of fish, his steady hand carefully noting them in the boat's log.

Tired, I leaned against the railing, zoning out. I could feel the micro-sleep creeping up my bones, but I pushed it off, determined to stay alert. I knew accidents could happen if I wasn't focussed.

'What are you doing?' John snapped his fingers in front of me, snatching the line from my hands.

Nudging me aside, he pulled in a sizable snapper. It twisted and turned as it struggled to break free from the hook, and I watched as John held it to the beckoning sunrise, marvelling at its size.

'Wow-ee!' he exclaimed. Dad and Pete slapped the man on the back, smiles from ear to ear. 'You got the catch of the night. The others were throwbacks. Small snapper and the odd kahawai. But this is good.'

Dad finished off his beer. 'All mine mooched along, eating anything, and I couldn't nab a keeper.'

'Snapper don't see too well in the dark,' John said excitedly. 'This one must have regained its sight. Caught it in time.'

I stood around the men, feigning interest. When the fish was bagged, I slipped away down below. My room was a mess. The sheets on the queen-size bed had been pulled off. The shower filled with toilet rolls, wet, sticky paper pressed against the tiles like papier-mâché. The small closet door was open, with my clothes strewn out all over the floor. The cushions in the corner lounge overturned. I looked towards the ornamental mirror, terror flooding my body. The words were written in lipstick, the same bubble-gum pink shade my mother wore.

The mirror made me do it.

Stumbling backwards, I steadied myself on the counter and looked into the mirror, gasping as my eyes locked to the pair of boots sticking out from under the blankets on the top bunk. Heart thudding, I slowly turned around, realising the boots belonged to Aaron.

'You know, when I first told Pete to buy the mirror, I didn't know it had come from the old lighthouse,' dad said. He slunk into the room, boots squelching.

'Someone mentioned it to me at the pub, about the lighthouse, and the mirror came up. An old, half-crazy caretaker told me the story about people seeking shelter in the lighthouse only to find their own deaths. I thought how curious it was that an object so unassuming could harness so much terror in someone. Sort of like you and fish.'

I stared at dad, at the tall, bulky man. I had tried so hard not to make a fool of myself in front of his friends. I had kept my jealously of Aaron to myself for so many years. The fisherman whose son can't fish. What a joke. Gasping, I stared into his hard eyes, my jolted mind trying to unravel what he was telling me. I was tired and confused, and all I wanted to do was sleep.

'But you know,' dad continued, 'seeking shelter from a storm isn't the best thing to do. I thought putting you in this room would persuade you to kill yourself. To slit your wrists with a fishing knife. You'd become so delirious without sleep you'd hook your eyes open to stay awake in your attempt to impress me. You'd be so tired you'd fall off the boat and drown.' He shrugged, spreading his big, bloodied hands. 'I read the stories of the people who claimed the mirror urged them to commit suicide. Perhaps it was haunted, like the park. Pete told you about the park, didn't he? About Pumpkin

Point?'

I nodded mutely, not bothering to mention it was Aaron, not Pete.

'Oh, it was swampy all right. Men could make careers out of undertaking. All those bodies from the old lighthouse.'

I shook my head, clenching and unclenching my fists.

'Those were ordinary people,' I muttered. 'The first people to settle in Cleveland. They were buried there because there was no other cemetery.'

Dad raised his finger, signalling my silence. 'Ah! They were buried there because they had been inside the lighthouse. They had sought shelter from the storm in a small cosy room. They had gathered there together, hoping to wait it out. They were buried there because they were cursed. Everyone told stories of the haunted lighthouse. Nobody spoke about the mirror,' he said, his voice growing louder. 'Death by suicide. An unspeakable act, back in the day. You surely wouldn't be going to heaven.'

'Now the ghosts haunt the mirror?' I mumbled inaudibly, remembering Aaron's words. 'Egging them on.'

'To join them,' dad said, eyes gleaming. 'And it's only a matter of time before you do the same. Because you're weak, easily misled, and I never loved you.'

He stepped forwards, and I pressed myself against the counter, eyeing the door.

'Look around you, Lucian. There's no escape.'

Dad removed his raincoat and laid it on the floor in front of him. Outside, dribbles of rain splattered on the window like blood, blossoming as the wind pressed against the glass.

'What are you going to do?'

I listened for the distant sounds of the rain, of the thunder, but the air had quietened to a dull lull of restless air and listless bird squawks.

'Tell me what you're going to do, dad.'

Dad stared through the window behind me, looking at the

brimming oranges and yellows in the sky. The weather was serene. They'd found shelter at last.

'I've bought another place,' he said matter-of-factly, digging his hand into the side pocket of his coat.

'And?'

He pulled out a small pistol, and I recognised it as my mother's Luger. She'd had it ever since Port Arthur, back in 1996. She'd moved from Eaglehawk Neck to Brisbane and met dad a few years later, and they'd had me. But she'd never got rid of the gun, and I was never allowed to use it.

'Why do you have mum's gun?'

'This is how it's going to be, Lucian.'

He snapped back the safety, his hands steady, eyes pugnacious and stern.

'You can't sleep. You can't fish. You can't even hold a fish, or gut a fish. You're an insomniac freak who constantly disappoints me. You know how much you embarrass me, Lucian? How hard it was to get these men out to sea with me? Your entire existence is a joke. Nobody wants to go deep-sea fishing with a man who can't even convince his son to take the trade.'

Tears ran down my cheeks as I struggled to hold back my anger.

'How could I learn from you?' I shouted hoarsely. 'You're busy with Aaron! You told him about me and Sarah! You're a hypocrite!'

Dad paused, thumb on the trigger. 'What are you rambling about? Who's Aaron?'

'Don't be an arsehole, dad! Not now. Not with me. You wish I was Aaron. You wish I loved fishing like he does. Don't lie!'

'You're a nutcase, Lucian! Who the fuck is Aaron? One of your make-believe friends? Get a grip!'

'Why don't you get a grip?' I shouted, mind whirring. 'You think I'm a failure! Why don't you shoot me?'

47

'Shoot you?'

'Shoot me in the face!'

'In the face?'

I rolled my eyes in exasperation. 'You're the one with the gun!'

'You're demented!'

'You're a liar! You're trying to make me think I'm crazy!'

'You *are* crazy!'

A bolt of thunder cracked against the window and I jumped, dropping the gun. Gasping, I stared at my shaking hands, wondering how it had transferred from dad to me so fast. Another micro-sleep, Lucian! Thunder rattled the room once more. I was a fool to think the storm had abated. Perhaps it had been there all along, and the morning thunder was a wakeup call, a warning.

I thought back to Aaron's earlier words. 'Thunderstorms, rain. Do you ever think they're supposed to wash us away?' he'd asked. 'Are they supposed to drench us so we become nothing but a smudge in a Monet masterpiece?' I thought back to our earlier conversation, when he'd been trying to intimidate me. 'You know, fish are sensitive when it comes to the weather. They sense changes in water pressure. Insects flitter when it's sprinkling, buzzing around, enticing the fish to the surface. They seem to lure the fish, as if they know they're making them more susceptible to being caught. Rain makes humans head indoors, but not here, out in the ocean. Not fish. When it rains, the fish come out to play. And the humans are ready…'

Had I somehow not sensed the change in my dad? Was he the insect luring me, the fish? Was the mirror the web? Had he been lying in wait all this time? Had he been the oncoming storm? The questions flooded my addled mind. There was no one on the boat I could trust, and no place to seek shelter. I was all alone.

'I want to stay down here, out of the storm!' I pleaded. 'I'm not a fisherman. I can't stand the rain. I can't stand the rotten

48

smell of the fish.'

'That's right! You're not a fisherman,' he jeered, snatching up the gun. 'You should kill yourself.'

Aaron moved to stand behind dad. The rest of the men had gathered around, telling us both to calm down. Aaron remained still, a presumptuous smirk on his face. For a moment, the clouds dissipated, and I saw Aaron move aside to stand in front of the mirror. I gasped, almost dropping the gun as I saw my reflection.

'Did you bring that here?' I shouted.

'You dragged it here yourself,' dad pleaded. 'Half-crazed. We thought you were sleepwalking. Shouting about some haunted lighthouse. That the mirror held ghosts. You're sick. Your mum wanted us to bond so you'd get better.'

I pressed my hands to my temples. What was going on? Was Aaron a ghost? Had he been in the lighthouse?

'Pete! You said you'd sliced open your arm after seeing it happen in the mirror!'

Everyone stared at me, mouths open. Thomas covered his mouth in shock, shook his head, and sprinted under deck. Dad slowly shook his head.

'Lucian. Pete killed Aaron in the lighthouse. Then he slit his own throat with a fishing knife. Remember? He left you a note. *The mirror made me do it.*'

'What? I looked over at Pete, at his straight back, his bushy eyebrows. While all the men were soaked, he appeared dry. But that makes no sense...Gasping, I watched as Aaron took a step back and passed through the mirror, disappearing. The sky was pink and clear.

Pressing the gun to my head, I pulled the trigger.

The Murder at Karreg Du
Cameron Trost

Wind shook Oscar Tremont's black Peugeot 403 as the vintage car advanced at a prudent speed. Over the trees lining the narrow back road, dark clouds raced like celestial stallions and rain fell in waves, the volleys of unseen archers opening battle. Leaves struck the windscreen, where they remained momentarily, until a sweep of the wipers sent them hurtling into the night. Following what was little more than a sealed lane in such conditions demanded the driver's undivided attention.

'I'm not so sure about your shortcut, Oscar. Have you noticed you have a knack for transforming relaxing weekends away into treasure hunts, rescue missions, and historical investigations?'

'There's a definite trend,' he replied, shooting her a mischievous glance.

'The storm's growing. I do hope we arrive soon.'

He said nothing, and they went back to listening to the baying of the wind.

'I've just lost my internet connection, so I can't navigate at all now.'

'We shouldn't be far from Le Gâvre. This road cuts through the forest, close to where we had a picnic with your parents years ago. Once we're out of the woods, we'll get back onto the departmental road.'

'Watch out!' Louise yelled, but he was already easing the car to a standstill.

Two yellow hazard lights were blinking at them through the darkness, and the fainter reflection of two others could be seen on the rough surface that blocked the road in front of the car.

Having come to a complete stop, the full force of the gale could be better appreciated. The Peugeot was being jostled and the branches all about them were thrashing maniacally.

'A fallen tree,' Louise mused. 'I suppose I ought to be surprised.'

'I assure you it wasn't me, chérie. Believe it or not, I was looking forward to an uneventful weekend.'

Oscar stared through the windscreen, lost in thought for a moment, before taking a heavy torch from the glove box and his fisherman coat from the back seat. He then braced himself for the sortie.

He retreated to the car a minute later.

'Your report?'

'The tree has been uprooted, almost certainly by the wind. There is no indication of human interference, such as the kind of marks an axe or saw would have made. It's dead, and some sections of the trunk appear to be rotten and hollow, but it would still be impossible to move without the help of Napoleon's Grande Armée. The vehicle is a recent model Audi with Parisian plates. The occupants, probably a couple, although their remarkable cleanliness renders the identification of conclusive clues difficult, have presumably sought shelter for the night.'

'We should follow suite. It's too late to head back now in the middle of a storm, and I don't fancy sleeping in the car.'

'Follow suit,' Oscar corrected her.

'Whatever.' She rolled her eyes. 'I wonder where they went.'

'There's a drive just past the tree, and a sign I can't quite make out from here.'

Louise gave her husband a stern look, and he pretended not to be enjoying the dramatic turn of events.

'Unless there's a spa resort at the end of that drive, you owe me another weekend away in the very near future.'

They shook on it.

Oscar edged the car up to the tree and parked beside the Audi. He took Louise's fisherman coat from the back seat and helped her into it, then hurried to the boot and grabbed their overnight bags.

After hoisting Louise over the tree, Oscar clambered across with the bags. They struggled against the howling wind and ignored the piercing rain as they pushed each other towards the gravel drive.

Oscar pointed his torch at the trembling sign just long enough to make out the words *château* and *chambres* as they hurried along. The ground rose, but dense forest and huge rocks protected them from the storm, and they soon found themselves at the top of a craggy hill, staring in disbelief at what was beyond doubt not a spa resort.

Perched atop the black hill was a small but foreboding castle. Its walls were dark and crenellated, but warm light beckoned from narrow windows and vehicles were parked in what had probably once been the stables.

Louise dashed across to the polished oak door and knocked five times, before noticing the electric doorbell. She jabbed the button with her thumb.

While they waited for a response, Oscar studied the stronghold, musing that it was undoubtedly one of the area's best-kept secrets. But his train of thought was promptly interrupted. A dull grating sound cut through the howling wind, followed by the sharp click of a far more modern locking mechanism, and the door swung open soundlessly to reveal two elderly women with heart-shaped faces and identical smiles.

'Welcome to Karreg Du. Step inside before you catch your death.'

Louise and Oscar followed the châtelaines into the entrance hall, where the warm air and echo of cheerful conversation coming from upstairs put them at ease.

'We have room to spare tonight. My name is Séverine, and this is my sister, Soazig.'

'Oscar and Louise. It's a pleasure to meet you, and we're very grateful for your welcome.' His French was eloquent, with just a vague hint of foreignness.

'Your stay will be completely free of charge, of course,' Soazig informed them.

'That's very kind of you, but quite unnecessary,' Oscar replied.

'We insist!' they chimed.

'The road is blocked and it's out of the question for us to take advantage of your dilemma,' Séverine said. 'We won't accept a single euro from you tonight. Of course, if you manage to find some pleasure in the predicament, you're always welcome to stay with us again in the future, under more propitious circumstances.'

'Thank you,' Louise said. 'It sounds like your other guests are enjoying themselves.'

'So they ought to be. We have a fire in the hearth, a pot-au-feu beside it, and a well-stocked cellar. The guestrooms are on the second floor. I'll show you to yours and then you can come down to the dining room on the first floor when you're ready. All our rooms have ensuites, so feel free to have a warm bath or shower if you like before joining us.'

Such sound advice could hardly be ignored, and once they had taken a change of clothes from their overnight bags and laid them on the king-size bed, Louise ran a warm bath while Oscar inspected the room; an admirable marriage of rustic Breton charm and modern comfort. The walls were of dark stone and the partition between the chamber and the bathroom was made of the same hardwood as the floor. A selection of tasteful landscape paintings unobtrusively adorned the walls.

If they hadn't been so hungry, they would have stayed in the bathtub much longer. Once the warm water had chased all trace of chill from their bodies, they hastily dressed and ventured down to the dining room.

'Have a seat,' Séverine said, indicating the two rush chairs that had been prepared for them.

Soazig carried their plates to the fireplace, beside which the pot-au-feu was being kept warm in a hefty three-legged pot.

Six guests sat around the table and each welcomed the newcomers in French, although Oscar recognised the English accents of two of them.

'What a wild night it has turned out to be!' Soazig announced conversationally, returning to the table with two steaming plates. 'As you can see, we've already eaten and are enjoying a glass of wine. Séverine, be a darling and pour them a drop while we introduce ourselves.'

They felt a little uncomfortable eating by themselves, but under the circumstances, the usual dictates of etiquette had to be ignored. Sensing their awkwardness, the other guests wished them a *bon appétit* and smiled encouragingly.

Oscar and Louise tasted their meals and assured the sisters that the dish was delicious.

Soazig gestured towards the retired couple, who were doing a fine job of not appearing to be overly confused.

'British?' Oscar ventured, speaking in their shared native tongue.

'Spot on!' the husband replied, clearly pleased to have a fellow English speaker present. 'I'm Richard and my wife's name is Emily. We're from Plymouth, just across the old Manche, as they call it here. How about yourselves?'

Oscar introduced himself and Louise, hoping that Richard wouldn't start talking about cricket when he told him he originally hailed from Australia.

He didn't, instead commenting on how the mood swings of the Atlantic must be a shock to the system for one used to sunnier climes. 'Go ahead and introduce yourselves to everybody in French. We'll try to follow.'

'We'll chat together later,' Louise assured the couple. 'I don't want to get rusty.'

Soazig, appearing to understand the gist of the exchange,

told Oscar and Louise the couple would certainly appreciate the chance to speak in English. She then continued with the introductions.

'This is Carole. She's a painter who comes here every year to find inspiration. Her work is enchantingly abstract, encouraging the beholder to interpret and contemplate according to his own perspective. We purchased two of her pieces for our library, which you will find at the end of the hallway on the third floor.'

Carole nodded appreciatively in response to Soazig's words. Her hazel eyes, flowing auburn hair, amber necklace, and patchwork dress in autumnal shades came together so harmoniously.

'It's a pleasure to make your acquaintance, despite the circumstances.'

'I'm sure this weather will inspire you,' Louise said.

'It already has,' Carole replied, glancing towards the nearest window, which was protected by rattling shutters.

'Anaïs is interested in local history,' Soazig said, referring to the woman next to Carole.

She wore a loose-fitting grey jumper and her long chestnut hair had hints of grey that accentuated her silver jewellery. As she raised a glass to the Tremonts, Louise admired her wolf ring and triskel bracelet.

'I share your interest in bygone days,' Oscar told her. 'I'm surprised I hadn't heard of Karreg Du before now.'

'A hidden gem, isn't it?'

'Every neck of the woods needs its secrets,' Séverine declared, winking at Oscar. 'The name of the castle stems from its geography, or rather, its geology.'

'Yes, I guessed as much,' Oscar told her. 'Gomz a ran un tammig brezhoneg.'

He was met with blank faces, and Louise rolled her eyes.

'I speak a little Breton,' he explained.

The others ummed and ahhed, quite impressed.

'We really ought to speak the old language,' Séverine admitted. 'It was our grandparents' mother tongue, but it was strictly forbidden when they went to school.'

'Would you like seconds?' Soazig asked, already on her feet.

Oscar and Louise assured her they had eaten enough, raising their palms in polite protest and then patting their stomachs in perfect conjugal concurrence.

The introductions had almost come full circle. There remained but one couple, seated on the other side of the sisters. They were middle-aged, smartly dressed, and, despite their attempts at appearing convivial, clearly disappointed that their plans for the evening had been interrupted.

'This is Anne-Laure and Laurent,' Soazig said.

'Vincent,' the woman corrected her.

'I am sorry.'

'Not at all,' he replied indifferently.

'Yours is the Audi, I take it?' Oscar asked.

'Yes,' Vincent said sharply, his attention caught. 'We were taking a shortcut, much like yourselves, I presume, but it turned out to be the wrong decision, didn't it? I almost drove straight into that damned tree trunk. What was the scene like when you were down there?'

Oscar held his tongue, which was eager to make a quip about Parisians behind the wheel.

'It was still blowing a gale, but your car was fine. Moving that fallen tree is going to require quite an effort.'

'At least we're all safe and sound in here,' Carole said.

'We really owe you a debt of gratitude,' Louise added.

'That's enough of that,' Soazig insisted, wagging a finger at the assembly. 'Your glasses are almost empty. I'll fetch some more wine. The men might prefer something stronger. We have cognac, don't we, Sév?'

'I have a bottle of whisky,' Oscar announced. 'Aberfeldy.'

'Good show, my man,' Richard congratulated him in English.

Oscar looked at the women, for he didn't share the sisters' antiquated assumption that no member of the fairer sex could possibly appreciate a fine drop of the peaty potion. But they shook their heads. Vincent also shook his head, rather disapprovingly.

'I'll be back in an instant,' Oscar told Richard, and turning to the sisters, he requested two whisky glasses if they wouldn't mind.

Anne-Laure remembered the expensive champagne from her cousin's cellar in Reims stashed away in her overnight bag but decided not to mention it. She was waiting for the appropriate moment to announce that the long drive from Paris and the dash through the storm had made them quite tired and that they were eager to get some rest. Indeed, she was just about to enunciate words to that effect when the chime of the doorbell rang out.

'The storm claims another victim,' Anaïs said.

Louise glanced at the grandfather clock standing guard close to the communicating door with the kitchen. It was a quarter to ten. Soazig appeared from the doorway carrying two bottles of wine and frowning.

'I'll get it,' Séverine called to her sister, already hurrying to the door.

She came back accompanied by a young man wearing a drenched pea coat. Both of them were smiling.

'It's Pierre,' Soazig gasped upon recognising him. 'We'd been wondering when we would see you next. You really ought to come more often.'

'I know I should. It's just that I don't get away from Tours much outside of university holidays, and I've been doing research as well as lecturing this semester. I've come down on urgent family business. I'll tell you all about it later. This storm is absolutely raging, isn't it? And I don't think it's going to ease off any time soon. There's a tree blocking the road, as I guess you know, so I had to run all the way up the drive. I was

57

intending to stop here, of course, but not necessarily for the night.'

'Storm or no storm, we wouldn't have it any other way.'

'I'll have to see what can be done about that tree in the morning. There are two other cars parked down there.'

'Let me take your coat, Pierre. Sit down by the fire. Have you eaten?'

'Thank you. I'm cold and tired, but not hungry.' He took his place and said good evening to the assembly.

The sisters introduced the new arrival, the son of dearly departed friends. Their families had known each other for generations.

'Pierre is a lovely young man,' Soazig concluded, glancing cheekily from Carole to Anaïs. 'He's a professor of French literature and is also versed in art and history.'

'Thank you, Aunt Soazig,' he replied curtly. 'That's enough now.'

Oscar arrived a moment later. 'We might need a third whisky glass,' he suggested.

'A glass of whisky would do just the job,' Pierre confirmed. 'Stay where you are, Soazig. I know where to find the glasses.'

The storm gave no sign of waning. The shutters went on shaking and the wind kept wailing in the chimney as the guests chatted and drank.

The next time Louise looked at the clock, it was almost eleven. The Parisians had retired to their room, eager to bring their unplanned evening to a close, as had Pierre, explaining that he didn't feel very well and had almost certainly had too much to drink.

Oscar was engaged in conversation with the English couple, but it was clearly past their bedtime. Louise gave him a gentle nudge and closed her eyes for a second when he looked at her.

'Quite right. We really ought to get some sleep,' he conceded.

The couple agreed, and the four women, overhearing them,

gave signs of being ready to follow suit.

They all lent a hand at clearing the table and bid each other a sound night's sleep.

#

Louise fell asleep with ease, cocooned in soft bedding, while Oscar listened to the rattling and whistling of the relentless wind. His eyes were closed and his mind wandered as he let the inharmonious lullaby carry him where it would. How long he had been in bed or whether he had slept at all, he couldn't say, but a sharp cry from within the castle reached his ears and made his eyes snap open.

'Louise?' he whispered.

No reply.

He was still trying to decide what to make of it when a gasp came from the corridor. It wasn't as loud this time, but it was more palpable now that he was fully awake.

He jumped out of bed and opened the door to find one of the sisters standing in the dark, as still as a statue, staring into the bedroom next to his. Taking a step closer, he saw that it was Séverine, and the dreadful look on her face precluded any ambiguity as to what she had discovered.

As she turned to him, he placed a reassuring hand on her shoulder. Her mouth was open, but she was incapable of a uttering a word.

'Go to your sister,' he told her firmly. 'Tell her what has happened.'

She walked away slowly, seeming to glide in her full-length nightgown, and followed the corridor to the left.

Oscar stepped into the room.

The bedside lamp was on, and its glow revealed the identity and condition of the room's occupant. It was Pierre, the professor, and he was dead.

On the bedside table, standing theatrically under the

lamplight, were an empty glass and an overturned bottle of sleeping pills, of which only a half dozen remained.

'Overdose?' asked Vincent, rushing across to the bedside.

'Don't disturb the scene,' Oscar warned.

The Parisian gave him a dirty look. 'I'm a doctor, and you're no gendarme.'

He checked Pierre's vital signs.

'Too late,' he said, stepping back. 'Much too late.'

There was growing commotion in the corridor as the other guests began to arrive, bleary-eyed and confused.

'The chap didn't top himself, did he?' Richard asked.

Oscar shrugged. 'It looks that way here, but it certainly didn't earlier this evening.'

Richard frowned.

'There's no signal.' Vincent was waving his phone in the air, while the roaring storm mocked him.

'I'll try mine,' Anaïs said, and hurried back to her room.

Anne-Laure wasn't having any success with her phone.

'He died over an hour ago,' Vincent announced. 'It would be folly to risk our own lives by venturing outside in this weather. There's nothing else to be done tonight. We'll have to wait until morning to inform the authorities, depending on when the wind subsides and when we can get that confounded tree off the road.'

They were silent for a minute and simply stared at the body in disbelief.

'What happened to him?' Louise asked, directing the question to her husband.

Vincent took it upon himself to answer. 'All the signs point to an overdose of sleeping pills.'

Oscar was on his knees, reaching between the bedside table and the wall.

'I've found a notepad,' he announced, holding it above his head for all to see and discreetly observing everybody's reactions. Only the sisters were not present in the room.

60

The spiral notepad had slipped down the narrow gap between table and wall. Oscar had seen the three letters hastily scribbled before showing the others. Although he didn't know what they meant, he'd immediately understood that it was the desperate message of a dying man who had come to a realisation too late. It was not a carefully considered suicide note.

Lou

'Lou?' Richard read aloud.

Vincent turned to Louise. 'It would appear he tried to write your name just before he died. Do you have any idea why?'

'That's quite an assumption. Those three letters could mean anything,' Oscar cut in.

'The man's final act before passing from this world was to force his hand to jot those letters on his notepad. That seems significant to me.'

'There is another explanation,' Oscar assured everybody. 'There must be.'

The other guests looked unconvinced. They held their tongues, but their eyes were accusatory.

'He was ill when he went to his room,' the doctor reminded Oscar. 'Therefore, it may not have been the sleeping pills that caused his death.'

The others listened, not knowing what to think or say.

'I appreciate that, but Louise has never met this man before, and has been with me all night. Isn't that so, darling?'

'Of course. This has nothing to do with me.'

Soazig and Séverine entered the room, doing their utmost to keep themselves together and carry on performing their role of unfaltering hosts.

'At any rate,' Soazig said, 'we need to wait the storm out and call the authorities in the morning. Nobody is to try to leave the castle tonight. Can we agree upon that?'

Everybody agreed.

Oscar looked at the word written on the notepad again.

'Let's all retire to our rooms until morning,' Soazig suggested.

'You won't try to leave, will you?' Vincent asked Oscar and Louise sternly.

'We will most certainly do nothing of the kind.'

'I think it would be best if the notepad remained in my possession.'

'Why would you think that?' Oscar replied. 'I'd much rather any other member of our party kept it.'

'Very well. Our hosts?'

'That's more reasonable,' Oscar agreed.

'Come on now,' Séverine insisted. 'Please go back to your rooms. I'll lock the door behind us.'

As soon as they were back in their room, Oscar poured himself a glass of Aberfeldy, installed himself in the armchair and closed his eyes, listening to the howling wind.

Louise lay awake in bed, bewildered and deeply worried. She had been accused of murder. That was what it boiled down to, wasn't it? Would the police jump to the same conclusion the other guests had. Was she to be arrested in the morning, once contact with the outside world had been re-established?

Twenty minutes later, Oscar finished his second glass of whisky and turned to her.

'The wind is still howling, as though it's trying to tell us something.'

'Your moustache is twitching, Oscar.' There was relief in her voice.

'Relax, my dear. They'll not lock you away.'

'You've worked it out?'

'All will be revealed in the morning. The murderer will stay put, along with everybody else. Escape would be self-incrimination. Our opponent is clever, but too confident.

Despite failing to notice the notepad when the sleeping pills were deposited on the bedside table, the murderer's confidence will remain intact, simply because our attention was so naïvely drawn to you and the real significance of those three letters is so far from anybody's mind.'

'He wasn't writing my name?'

'Of course not. The chap was a professor of literature.'

Oscar switched the lamp off.

'I don't see the relevance.'

'You will,' he assured her, getting into bed. 'We need to get some sleep before tomorrow's performance. Sweet dreams, Lou.'

She felt like slapping him, but instead kissed him goodnight.

#

Nobody slept soundly that night, not even once the storm had died in the grey hours before dawn. They lay in their beds, staring vaguely at the ceiling or keeping both eyes fixed on their locked bedroom doors. Oscar was gently caressing Louise's hair. She trusted him, but that didn't prevent her from feeling distressed. She was the prime suspect in the murder, if that's what it really was, and would remain so until Oscar had elucidated the problem and exposed the killer. Of course, the police would be called as soon as somebody got phone reception, and there was no knowing what they would make of it all.

She turned to him, without raising her head from the pillow, so that he could keep caressing her hair.

'I know what happened. Don't worry.'

'Can you prove it?'

'If the murderer is as confident as I think, it's a closed case. If I'm wrong, we'll have to go over the castle from top to bottom.'

'Won't you tell me who it is?'

Oscar's moustache twitched.

Louise sighed, but it turned into a soft laugh.

'You won't tell me what the murderer might have tried to dispose of either?'

'It amounts to the self-same question,' he added, and that was the only hint she would be given.

Footsteps echoed in the hallway, and Oscar knew who it was and where he was heading. He got out of bed, rubbed his face and stroked his moustache, and opened the bedroom door.

'Good morning,' Vincent said, trying to peer into the bedroom. Oscar didn't step out of the way.

'My wife is here. She's had a rather unpleasant night, unaccustomed as she is to being accused of murder.'

'It's not a matter of pointing fingers. There are just facts to be stated. I've managed to get through to the police and they'll be here very soon, so it's out of our hands now.'

'Excellent,' Oscar replied. 'We should prepare ourselves for their arrival.'

Vincent raised his eyebrows. 'Whatever do you mean by that?'

'The police would surely appreciate it if we solve the crime for them.'

Vincent laughed, but there wasn't a trace of joy in it.

'You think you've solved the crime and can clear your wife's name?'

Oscar nodded. 'All I need is to have everybody together in the same room. How about the library? We'll have a strong coffee and I'll tell you what happened.'

Vincent was speechless.

'It's better than moping around in our rooms all morning.'

'If everybody is willing, I see no problem with your idea. I'm curious about this little show of yours. I want to see how you play detective.'

'I don't play detective any more than you play doctor, my friend.'

64

'Oh, I see. You're a private eye.'

'That's one way of putting it. Let's get moving. Nobody will refuse coffee in the library, I'm sure.'

Fifteen minutes later, they were all together, sipping the rich brew Séverine had prepared. Everybody did their best to seem relaxed and suitably solemn. The sisters were the only ones whose red eyes and streaked cheeks bore witness to a night of tears. They sat on the library's two leather armchairs, with the women standing close by them. Richard was looking at Oscar thoughtfully, waiting for the whole affair to be cleared up, and Vincent was leaning against the wall by the window, clear daylight playing on his analytical face.

Oscar glanced around the room, noting every detail, then looked down at his clasped hands. He breathed a sigh of relief.

'The police are on their way, and when they get here, Pierre's murderer will be handed over.'

Everybody gasped appropriately, including the murderer.

'How do you know?' Soazig asked.

'I didn't introduce myself entirely honestly last night. I am an investigator of strange and inexplicable occurrences, and what happened last night is almost inexplicable; almost, but not quite. Pierre's note indicated that he didn't commit suicide, but it had nothing to do with my wonderful wife. We'll get back to that in a minute.'

Confused faces watched Oscar.

'Séverine and Soazig, I need you to confirm the motive for me. Nobody here knew Pierre except you and the murderer.'

The sisters looked around nervously.

'Please tell us why he came home this weekend. Is there an inheritance dispute in his family?'

The sisters' eyes widened.

'That's precisely why,' Soazig confirmed. 'His parents are both dead, and the property, which is considerable, is under dispute. Pierre has one brother, from whom he has been estranged for years. He never wanted to share just what happened between them with us, but there was bad blood.'

'What does that have to do with any of us?' Soazig asked. 'These people are strangers.'

'So it would seem,' Oscar continued. 'It is not, however, really the case.'

Murmurs filled the library and everybody glanced sideways at each other. Oscar observed each of them, making sure not to focus on the murderer, who was becoming increasingly alarmed.

'One of us stands to inherit the estate?' Vincent asked.

'Precisely. With Pierre out of the way, having taken his own life, as we were supposed to assume from this well-staged performance, his brother would inherit everything. Unfortunately, the notepad was overlooked. That one clue ruined the act.'

'Why did he write *lou*?' Louise asked.

'It has nothing to do with you; I knew that straight away. Pierre was a professor of literature, and no professor, not even in the throes of death, would begin a name with a lowercase letter. It was a common noun he'd been trying to write when death stilled his hand. Perhaps the notepad slipped off the bedside table before he could finish.'

The audience was dumbstruck.

'I suspected he'd remembered something that had struck him as being out of place; had realised some detail that would incriminate the murderer. He was a terribly clever fellow, for not only did he reveal the identity of the murderer in his final moment, but also the modus operandi.

'Last night, in my room, I went through every word in the French language beginning with those three letters, and while I did that, I listened to the storm. It was the howling wind that gave me the answer.'

Oscar waited for somebody to say the word, but only the murderer knew it, and her lips remained tight.

'The howling wind made me think of *loup*,' he explained.

'Wolf,' he added for the benefit of the English couple.

'The ring!' Carole shouted eventually, and pointed at Anaïs.

Anaïs understood the game was up and made a dash for the door, but Louise was quick to react and tackled her. Together they slammed into a bookshelf, sending numerous leather-bound volumes plummeting to the floor.

Carole sprang over to help Louise.

'Splendid tackle, Louise,' Oscar said. 'The French rugby team could do with your help.'

The assembly was too stunned to laugh at his quip. The men watched on as Louise and Carole held Anaïs firmly by the arms.

'Carefully remove the wolf ring from her finger and pass it to me,' he told Louise, walking over to the three women.

He held the ring up so that everybody could see it, then lowered it to the level of his chin and held it at arm's length. He pulled on the wolf's head and it flipped open to reveal an empty receptacle.

'A poison ring?' Séverine rasped, scowling at Anaïs.

'She must have poisoned him in cold blood while we were sharing a glass last night!' Soazig snarled.

'My suspicions were first aroused when she led us to believe that she was single, but I'd noticed a pale band on her finger where a wedding ring was usually worn. That in itself is no crime, for it sometimes happens that married men and women pretend to be single for various reasons. Looking back, of course, it was far more significant than I'd imagined. There's no doubt in my mind that Anaïs is married to Pierre's estranged brother.'

The assembly gasped.

'You don't know that!' she hissed.

'I wonder whether Pierre realised who this wretched woman really was,' Séverine said sharply, looking daggers at Anaïs.

'There's no way of knowing as far as I can tell,' Oscar replied. 'It may have occurred to him as he breathed his final breath, when he recalled the wolf ring.'

'It really was awfully clever of him,' Séverine said admiringly, holding back the urge to cry. 'He always was a smart young man. Only, the thing is, if you hadn't been here, Oscar, this vile creature, Anaïs, or Lucrezia, or whatever her real name is, would have got away with it.'

Oscar spread his arms and shrugged.

'That may be so. It's often the plight of the highly intelligent to be too ingenious for their own good, making them seem the opposite of what they are to the unappreciative masses,' he stated discursively, clearly unaware of the supreme arrogance of his remark. 'Let's be generous. There is the slim possibility that the French police might have fumbled their way to the truth eventually.'

Vincent took a step forward, arms crossed and chin raised. He was doing his best to conceal the curious mix of admiration and jealousy written on his face.

'I envy your methodical mind, but there's one aspect to this crime that you may have overlooked; the fallen tree.'

'Yes, the tree. I examined it before seeking shelter last night. You mustn't envy my incessant suspiciousness and fertile imagination, I assure you. It's a burden. In any case, the tree was pure luck. Luck, I say, because without it, I wouldn't be here. The break appeared to be completely natural. There was no indication that it had been chopped or sawed. That wasn't a necessary part of the plan and would have risked attracting attention. Even though the brothers were estranged, naturally, they knew each other's ways. That Pierre preferred to visit his dear friends, Séverine and Soazig, rather than stay at the family home would have been evident to his brother.'

The sisters nodded their agreement.

'The brother is probably there as we speak,' Vincent suggested, 'practicing his reaction for when the news reaches him and getting ready to take on the role of lord of the manor.'

They all turned to Anaïs.

'Idle accusation,' she spat, not a whisper of remorse in her voice.

'The police will take care of all those formalities when they get here,' Oscar told her calmly. 'Your identity will be established, as will the identity of the poison which was held in this ring and which will be found in Pierre's body.'

Uneasy silence reigned in the library briefly, until the doorbell sounded, echoing through the castle with all the finality of a judge's gavel.

The Bells of St. Clement's
Stuart Olver

Alyce Benning allows herself to be pushed back slowly onto the moist carpet of moss and leaves between the giant buttresses of a booyong tree. All the while, Sandra's lips are against hers, and she savours their sweet saltiness. Her nostrils flare as Sandra presses against her fiercely, bringing smells of damp earth and decay, of soap and sweat. There are small twigs pressing into her back, but the discomfort registers only peripherally. Alyce's hand creeps up under Sandra's pleated skirt, even though they can still hear the sound of the school group, and it's all so illicit, all so delicious. If anyone were to double back, if anyone were to catch them, it'd be instant dismissal for her, certain expulsion for Sandra. It's insane, but she's in the mood for crazy. It's dangerous, dangerous like the thunder now growling somewhere above the dappling rainforest canopy that shrouds their indiscretion.

Alyce feels like they've slipped out of time, so she is not sure whether seconds or minutes have passed when Sandra finally lifts her head. The girl looks at Alyce, her eyes playful. 'Wouldn't you have finished explaining the life cycle of the giant stinging tree to me by now Ms. B? After all, that is the reason why we're lagging behind.'

'Ha! I'm giving you a thorough, hands-on demonstration. Honestly though, look at the two of us, rolling around in the mud.'

'Yeah, we're two crazy bitches, right?'

'That's not going to stop the leeches though.'

Alyce reluctantly eases Sandra away from her, and they stand and brush themselves off. She peeks around the tree and gives the thumbs up. 'Mr. Stratton has got them to the car park by now, I reckon. Time to go before we're missed?'

'You told Stratton we weren't coming back with him on the bus, didn't you?'

'Yeah, I signed you out. I'm walking you home for some extra tutoring. Your classmates might be wondering what's happened to us though.'

'Huh! None of them give a shit about me.'

'Oh, I wouldn't say that. They're probably just a bit intimidated because you're so magnificent.'

'Right. And don't you forget it!' laughs Sandra.

A cool breeze whittles its way through the fig trees and lilly pillies, pushing aside the warm blanket of air that until now draped the forest floor. Leaves stir restlessly across the canopy, and something wet and cold plops onto Alyce's cheek.

'I think I just felt my first raindrop,' she says. 'Smells like hail too, I reckon.'

'Don't say that.'

'Are you kidding? Doesn't the thought of large shards of ice scything out of the sky give you goose bumps?'

'You're insane, Alyce. You know that?'

'I don't give a fuck. I'm sick of playing it safe.'

Alyce watches as Sandra adjusts her blouse. There is such a wild beauty in the girl, such a fierce power in her lean body. And the insanity that she was playfully accusing Alyce of was surely equally shared between both of them. After all, it was Sandra who pushed them into places beyond wistful glances and furtive touches. Sandra who made her feelings abundantly clear when she pressed her teacher into a corner of the classroom after school a fortnight ago, one hand cradling her head while the other slipped under her blouse.

Alyce finds the path, and they increase their pace as thunder again rattles across the sky. Rain begins to *patter patter* on the arching fronds of piccabeen palms, and drifts down to moisten looping cordyline leaves that fringe the track.

'Did you notice Mr. Stratton giving you a few funny looks

71

during the walk?' asks Alyce.

'Can't say that I did.'

'You don't think he's on to us, do you?'

'Nah. He's just a dopey biology teacher. How someone as young as he is could be so obsessed with fungus, I don't know. I swear he spent most of the time looking at the ground...ah, here's the car park.'

They emerge from under the rainforest canopy into the open space, which is completely devoid of vehicles.

'Hey, where's the coach?' asks Alyce.

The excursion bus that brought the senior students to the Mount Tamborine national park is nowhere to be seen. Alyce strides forward and gazes up the road.

'You'd think they'd at least wait till we emerged safely,' she says.

'I told you, they don't care. Damn, I'm getting wet.'

The rain has intensified. Alyce fishes around in her backpack for her wet-weather jacket, and hands it to Sandra. The girl hadn't bothered to walk with one, and that was understandable. It was a muggy day.

'Your place is close to here, isn't it, Sandy? That wasn't a lie I told Richard Stratton, was it?'

'No, but I still don't think we're going to make it...Alyce, I'm really getting soaked.' Sandra's voice is tinged with concern.

'Let's get under that picnic shelter.'

They scamper across to the wooden table and bench, with its rough shingled roof. The breeze has stiffened and cooled, and Alyce shivers as rain spatters under the overhang. Over to the southwest, the darkening clouds have a green tinge.

'I don't like this, Alyce. What if it really starts to hail? There's a gallery or something over the road. Can't we shelter there?'

Alyce peers through the rain to a clearing cut out of the rainforest on the other side of the road. It appears to be the start of a broad drive that disappears down a slope. She can barely make out the words STUDIO - GALLERY written on a weather-beaten sign.

'Shouldn't we call your uncle? You live with him, don't you?'

'Now, why would I invite you back to my place, Honey, if I knew he'd be around?'

There is crackling like fire as a flurry of small hailstones bears down on the shelter. Alyce puts her hand on the girl's shoulder and looks up and down the deserted road.

'I guess we could shelter at the gallery till the storm passes over,' she says.

'Come on!'

And Sandra is away, sprinting towards the road. Alyce struggles to keep up with her, and keep her footing, as she aquaplanes across the streaming bitumen, and skids down the studio's drive. It ends in a small parking area, which fronts a windowless, timber-panelled building, screened by native ginger and sunk deep into the rainforest. The two of them reach the small verandah up a short flight of stairs and stand huffing and wiping rain from their faces and hair. Alyce has spent many hours exploring the various cafés, craft shops and galleries scattered throughout Mount Tamborine, but she doesn't think she has ever encountered one quite as scruffy-looking as this one.

'Is it even open?' she says, looking at the closed double doors.

Sandra steps forward and pushes against the left door. It swings inward.

'There's your answer.'

The lights are on inside, illuminating a small reception room which is surprisingly fresh-looking and presentable. A counter runs across one side, and a book and curio rack along the other. Some potted ficus and ferns break up the stark lines of the room, and a comfortable couch rests against one wall. At the far end there is a small passageway leading to some toilets, and an opening screened by a hanging curtain, which presumably leads into the gallery proper.

Alyce helps Sandra shrug out of her raincoat, then peers over the counter. There are a couple of empty chairs and a desk, which runs along the length of the counter at a lower level. It contains a calendar, and a computer with accompanying mouse pad and pencil jar, but little else. Alyce looks around in vain for a service bell or buzzer.

'I guess we just go through,' says Sandra, and before Alyce can stop her, she sweeps aside the curtain and disappears through the inner doorway.

'Wait, Sandra.'

Alyce hesitates, then walks back towards the main entrance. Hail is now thudding against the ground, and some of it is the size of golf balls. Lightning strobes somewhere above her, and churning clouds flee from its whip crack. It is quite obvious there will be no escape for some time yet. So she turns around, moves to the curtained opening, and joins Sandra on the other side. The girl is gazing around the room in astonishment.

The setting is stunning. Silken sheets descend vertically from rails in the ceiling, layer after layer, spiralling out from each other, swirling in sheer satin charmeuse and translucent organza whorls of ivory, peach, and mauve, carving the air in the room into sinusoidal passageways and burrows that radiate out from the centre. And illuminated by spotlights at the very core rests a white leather upholstered chaise longue, dazzling like a sacred heart.

'What is it?' asks Alyce.

'Some kind of artwork, I guess.'

They hear the lightning first, a snare drum crack that ignites the air and detonates a rolling cannonade across the clouds. The wind rages around the gallery, spitting hail against the eaves. The walls shudder as if the building itself is startled, and the lights flicker momentarily.

Sandra looks up at the ceiling. 'I hope the roof doesn't cave in!'

'It's unlikely,' says Alyce, more to convince herself than anything else. She moves around the display, and opens up, with every step, a different juxtaposition of form and space, at times masking and at times laying bare the sofa at the centre of the studio. Meanwhile, Sandra has walked towards another door at the side of the room.

'Hey, Alyce! Come here. You've got to see this.'

Alyce finds her standing just inside another room. Each of its windowless walls is dominated by bookshelves, which are tightly packed with the spines of innumerable tomes of all colours and thicknesses. The floor is occupied by a huge moulded foam rubber rendition of an opened book, raised at a slight angle, and with blank pages spread wide and covering several square metres. Four large moulded bells are positioned on the pages, and between the bells are a couple of baskets holding what look like oranges, with perhaps some lemons thrown in. There is a laptop resting on a small table, and a camera set high against the wall behind it. There is also a digital SLR mounted on a tripod near the table. The only other objects in the room are a rectangular case lying on the ground near one corner, and a candlestick and cigarette lighter placed on top of the case.

'What a great room, huh?' says Alyce, walking over to the nearest bookshelf. She scans some of the volumes, finding several handsome hardbacks dealing with nursery rhymes and fairytales, and wedged rather incongruously between them, a coffee table book of early twentieth-century nude photography.

'Let's see what's on the computer,' says Sandra.

'Hmm, maybe we shouldn't touch anything...'

But Sandra is already halfway towards the laptop. Alyce follows her, just as curious to determine the purpose of the large replica book taking up most of the floor space. There is a simple, geometric screensaver crawling around the computer

75

screen, so Sandra nudges the mouse. The desktop has a few of the standard browser and office icons, and one folder in the middle simply labelled PHOTOS. Sandra double-clicks the folder. It opens to display several rows of image thumbnails. She clicks on the first one.

A photograph fills the screen. It shows the open foam rubber book. More foam rubber in the shape of a green hill has been moulded onto the top half of the pages. A cut-out of a covered well is attached to the summit, and a painted sheet forms a sandy path running along the bottom. Large 3D lettering creeps down the side of the left page, and forms the words of the Jack and Jill nursery rhyme. Two real children have been positioned on the foam rubber and integrated into the scene: a boy, dressed in jacket and breeches, and holding a pail, sprawls at the base of the hill, while a girl, wearing a petticoat under her dress and a bonnet on her head, reaches out to him from halfway up the page. The effect is a startling likeness of a child's 3D pop-up book.

Sandra uses the mouse to scroll to the next image. This time, there are four children posed in a scene from Humpty Dumpty. One is dressed in an egg costume and sits towards the high edge of the giant book, on some foam rubber decorated like a stone wall. The other three children kneel at the base of the wall. They are dressed as toy soldiers, and gaze up at the egg with grim expressions on their faces.

'Quaint, hey?' says Sandra.

'That's one word you could use for it.'

'Happy family snaps with a twist. What d' you reckon?'

'Suppose so. I guess this place is more like a photographic studio than an art gallery.'

'Well then,' says Sandra with a wide grin, 'Where's the photographer hiding?'

She sashays away towards the foam rubber book, climbs up on the lower end, and flops down on her back near the centre crease.

'Wow! Comfortable,' she says, 'Okay, I'm ready for my shot.'

She raises herself on her elbows and brings one knee up. She smiles shyly in a way that Alyce has always found so bewitching. Her blouse, still damp from the rain, presses against her bra.

Twin serpents of desire and whispered guilt coil through Alyce. Sandra seems somehow vulnerable, lying there on the book, and for a moment, Alyce sees her student, not her lover. But why should she be torn between responsibility and desire? The two natures shouldn't be incompatible. *No*, thinks Alyce angrily, *I will not be defined so narrowly.*

'Oh, Sandy, you look...'

Lightning lashes the earth somewhere close outside, and the discharge is so intense that, for an instant, Alyce isn't sure whether the room itself hasn't cracked in two. Then she and Sandra and the book and the shelves are plunged into absolute darkness.

'My God! Sandra, are you OK?'

There is no answer.

'Stay where you are. I'll come and get you.'

Alyce starts inching across the floor.

'Sandy? Are you there? Answer me!'

Alyce thinks she hears a scuffling sound, faint footfalls, and the creak of a door. But is it merely the blustering wind, the shuddering of the eaves, the bow-strain of branches stretched to their limits?

'Sandy!' Her voice now a scream.

Alyce almost trips over the edge of the foam rubber. She drops to all fours, scrabbles across the softly yielding surface, sweeps her hands back and forth. She finds the midline of the giant book, where the surface curves sharply inwards. The place where Sandra had lain. There is no one there. She tries to crawl across the book in ever-widening circles, but her hands slap against the rubber bells. The darkness all around her teems with imagined forms. A thousand phantom hands surround her, their fingers stirring her goose flesh.

And then she remembers her smartphone.

Her mobile has been in her pants pocket all along. She can use its built-in torch. She pulls it out, and soon a diffuse cone of light is illuminating her immediate surrounds.

Apart from her, the room is empty.

'Sandra, where did you go?'

Alyce hops off the book, and walks steadily towards the first studio. She plays the beam over its silken whorls. They rise to the ceiling like the funnel-web of a monstrous spider. She circles around the display, pushes aside the curtain leading into the reception room, and peers out. The room is quiet and still.

It certainly wasn't beyond Sandra to turn this whole thing into a game. It was her idea to deliberately lag behind the group in the forest, and when she pushed Alyce down into the bushes, it came as a surprise. Perhaps she was hiding behind the counter at this very moment.

Alyce steps into the reception area, and quickly shines the light at the desk and floor behind the counter. Sandra is clearly not hiding there. Still, Alyce decides to check outside. She finds the handle on the front door and pulls, but it refuses to budge. She pushes against the solid wood without success. She shakes the handle and the door rattles against some sort of internal bolt.

'Damn it!'

She has been locked in.

'Sandy, are you out there?'

Alyce can hear nothing over the hissing of the rain and the dark growl of thunder high in the sky. She can't believe that Sandra would run off and leave her alone in the gallery. The locked front door is disconcerting, to be sure, but even that could perhaps have been the result of slamming in the wind. No, Sandra was still in here, and once Alyce found her, they'd figure out a way to get out.

Alyce makes her way back towards the book room, sweeping the light from her phone this way and that. Even so, smothering shadows seem to detach from the walls to sniff her out, and the air whispers to her of things that move just out of sight, parting and gathering behind her like the wake of a ship.

The laptop screen in the book room is still on, apparently running on battery power. As soon as Alyce steps up to it, the image on the screen changes, although she didn't move the mouse or tap any keys. Now, the scene depicted is of Little Miss Muffet being menaced by a large, black, rubber spider crawling down a page of the foam book. The real-life subject has her face turned away from the camera, and Alyce immediately feels that something is out of place. The girl is dressed in modern jeans and a blouse. Then the image changes subtly. The girl's face is now angled ever so slightly back towards the camera, although the projected scene remains static. The image changes again, and then once more, quickly. More of the girl's face becomes visible. It is clear the series of shots have been taken by a camera operating in burst mode; each picture is being replaced by the next so rapidly now that the girl's head is rotating as in a movie, and Alyce watches in mounting horror as she turns to look straight at the camera, her face set in a terrified mask.

It is Sandra. Unmistakably, unquestionably Sandra. But Sandra as she would have looked perhaps three years ago, when she was fourteen or fifteen.

Alyce gasps and shines her light on the large foam rubber book, despite the impossibility that she is watching something in real time. Sandra of course is not sitting there. The implication is like a cold hand closing around Alyce's heart. Someone is remotely manipulating the laptop.

The wan smartphone light is creating shadows rather than dispelling them. Alyce's hands start to shake, as a nasty suspicion begins to take root in her mind. Because the power is still out, the remote operator is most likely using a Bluetooth equipped smartphone to control the laptop. Alyce is sure Bluetooth can't have a range of more than ten metres or so. Whoever is scrolling through the photos is probably watching her at this very moment.

'Sandra, stop mucking around! Come out here where I can see you!'

The photo on the screen disappears. It is replaced almost immediately by the first frame of a video, which begins playing. Alyce's stomach clenches like a fist. The first studio is lit by a red glow, and the silken sheets surround the chaise longue like the petals of a rose. Something is happening on the central couch; a suppleness of movement, a subtle rhythm, a flexing of limbs. But the hanging fabrics conspire to obscure the nature of the beast, and tension like a silent scream builds in Alyce as she wills the camera to peer past the layers of silk. Then the camera begins to move gradually around the room to the right, while zooming in slowly towards the centre. Alyce wonders if she is imagining the back of a head, the muffled contours of a face. No, they are unmistakable. There are at least two bodies on the couch, straining against each other. She can't see their faces clearly, can't be sure...

The pale white beam from a spotlight suddenly caresses the lovers' forms, makes a cocoon of the surrounding flimsy material. A man's jawline is visible, his eyes scrunched shut, and his mouth half open. But there are no groans, no sighs; the video spools silently. The chaise longue is momentarily obscured as the camera angle plays with form and space, and then a woman's hips are glimpsed, rocking up and down. The man's head bobs up again, and Alyce has a brief clear view of his features, his mouth wide open as if emitting an ecstatic cry. Then the video stops playing and the screen returns to the desktop icons.

Almost immediately, Alyce's ears pick up a muffled sound from the other room. She starts back towards it, the torchlight tracing an erratic pattern over the floor and walls. Booming

80

thunder obliterates her footfalls. The building quakes as if in fear. This storm is not wearing itself out; if anything, it is intensifying, as if it is a petulant child that, having already lashed out in anger, finds shame and guilt driving it towards even greater fury. By now, an average South-East Queensland storm would have swept on out over the bay, having huffily dumped its load of ice and water before making a run for it. But rain is pummelling the roof with renewed vigour.

Alyce steps through the communicating door, and, even before she can cast her light around, it seems the air itself is telling her of the existence of something not present ten minutes ago, as if the space is a living entity whose remembered contours are altered somehow. Her hand shakes as she points her phone around the room, its light barely caressing the hanging sheets before dimly illuminating something lying upon the chaise longue in the centre. Alyce pushes her way through the mazelike layers of silk, her chest tightening as the sheets fall away behind her to reveal a large book lying on the lounge. Someone has taped an A3 print of a photograph onto its cover. Alyce shivers involuntarily as she recognizes the face of the man who'd been in the video.

Alyce begins to notice a faint, chemical smell. She leans in towards the book, and it is obvious the smell is coming from there. With trembling fingers, she grips the cover. But the book only opens towards the centre. The other pages have been glued together, and a shallow cavity has been carved out of them. She stares at the opened book for a second, her mind struggling to comprehend what she sees. The face of the man in the video has been filleted from his skull, and his formalin-fixed, pallid features stare out at her from the page.

'Do you like my 3D pop-up book?' calls a voice from the shadows. Alyce turns towards the sound, and a torch's powerful beam seems to dance as it slants this way and that between the hanging sheets, like something alive and serpentine for which the fabric is no real barrier.

'It's all part of the story, you see.'

Something in the tone of Sandra's voice causes icy fingers to run up and down Alyce's spine. She takes a half step backward, and tries to shield her eyes against the light to get a better view of the girl.

'Sandra, are...are you OK?'

'Never better. Though I don't mind admitting the storm threw me there for a moment. Of course, it did make it easier for me to tempt you in here. And then the lights went out unexpectedly, after weeks of careful planning. But the darkness actually did me a favour. Allowed me to get a little creative. So, come on out, and I'll show you some more.'

'I...I don't know if I want to.'

'Then I'll come in and get you.' Sandra angles her light down slightly so it illuminates a large carving knife in her other hand. She raises the weapon and slashes it across one of the silken sheets before her.

'Sandra, no!'

The girl giggles and slices through another hanging drape. She begins to move inwards.

Alyce's stomach clenches with fear. On the verge of panic, she stumbles away from the approaching student, trying to find a way through the suspended sheets that seem to cling to her like the strands of a spider's web. She twists around one, gets her feet tangled in another, and desperately grabs the fabric to stop herself from falling. She hangs, half suspended, organza wrapping around her, a trapped fly waiting for the approaching spider. She lifts her face to cry with fear and rage, and a fine water spray mists against her skin. The ceiling groans, and Alyce fancies she sees plaster fall in fine flakes like snow. Then something pops above her like a Christmas cracker, and the ceiling bulges inward and begins to crack. A second later, the whole edifice collapses around her. Sheets descend in a smothering mass, and a ceiling rail glances against her forehead. The ceiling yawns open like a heart valve, and rain sluices down where the roof has been ripped away.

Alyce collapses, dazed by the blow to her head. A wooden beam falls and pounds her lower arm, fracturing it, and the pain jerks her back towards full consciousness. She tries to stand, but flops onto her back as dizziness and nausea close on her again. Raindrops splatter against her face, obliterating her tears, and the eddying wind snatches the wail from her lips. Above her, the clouds press upon one another like coal rattling along a conveyor belt. In the half-light, she can just make out her smartphone, smashed beyond repair.

Alyce hears someone whimpering, and it is a few moments before she realises the sound is actually coming from her own lips. Her broken arm is throbbing, and moving it, even slightly, sends a hot electric shock through the limb. But she forces herself to carefully cradle it against her stomach, then rolls onto her side so that the rain is not directly splattering onto her face. Within seconds, Sandra, who is seemingly completely unharmed, has made her way to her teacher's side.

'Oh my, Alyce. Oh dear, oh dear, what are we going to do with you now?'

'Sandra, please...I think my arm's been broken.' Alyce can barely manage a whisper.

'I guess I'm going to have to move you myself. At least I won't need this now.' Sandra tosses the knife back towards where she's come from. She puts down the torch so that its beam is facing out in the same direction. Then she bends down, swiftly grabs Alyce under the shoulders, and, with an effort that brings a snarl to her lips, begins to pull Alyce through the debris. Alyce's mind seems to warp inside out, as excruciating pain spikes through her arm. She lingers on the edge of consciousness, only dimly aware of what is happening to her. Though she can feel herself sliding over sodden fabric, and her side bumps painfully against pieces of the ceiling, the path outwards seems not to be completely blocked. Somewhere deep in her mind, survival instincts are telling her to struggle, to resist, but any sort of movement seems beyond her, as she tries to steady her injured arm against Sandra's tugging.

Sandra drags Alyce through the door leading into the book room, and out of the rain. Then she pauses, and ducks back out quickly to grab the torch and knife. She places the torch on the floor, angling the light towards the large foam rubber book. Alyce has no time to react before Sandra is standing over her again.

'For God's sake, Sandra, why are you doing this?'

'Stories,' says the girl, and in that one word Alyce hears a breathlessness, a hunger, a catch in the throat like a predator spotting its prey for the first time. 'I love stories. I started telling you one earlier; a glimpse into my tale. Courtesy of what you saw on the laptop. But perhaps we should start further back. You see, I was raised as a permanent foster child by my uncle and aunt. My uncle really was the one who took care of me; my aunt and I never got along, and besides, she died when I was ten. It was my uncle who would read to me in bed every night, while my aunt sat on the couch drinking God-knows how many gin and tonics. It was through my uncle that I learned to love stories and reading. He started with nursery rhymes, and I've never forgotten them. I certainly had my favourites: Humpty Dumpty, Jack and Jill, Little Miss Muffet. It probably wasn't until I was five or six that I was able to understand what exactly it was about them that I liked. They were violent. There was suffering. Jack with his smashed head. And Jill wasn't spared either. Then there was the irreparable ruin of Humpty. And an innocent girl menaced by a spider, who may or may not have had sinister intentions.'

'Sandra, please...stop this. I need medical attention. If you have any feelings for me at all...' Alyce hears herself slurring, but can't seem to control her speech. She is finding it hard to focus; her mind is turbulent with rapid, disjointed thoughts.

'My uncle was a photographer,' says Sandra. 'He built this studio, and I've been maintaining it since his passing. He

84

started off doing weddings, then got into glamour photography: Valentine's Day shots, couples' fantasies, that sort of thing. But it was my idea to do a nursery rhyme room. Something different for the kids, you know. As I got older, I was helping my uncle more and more. Even modelling for him on each new nursery rhyme set we came up with. Eventually, I was doing almost all of the composing and shooting of the kids' portraits.'

Alyce is now shivering uncontrollably. It is not only pain and fear. Cold from her wet clothes has been seeping through her skin, soaking into her muscles. She must move. She has no choice. She inches herself around till she is facing Sandra. Water droplets are still running down the slick strands of the girl's hair and silently falling to the ground. The top button of her blouse has worked loose, and tiny beads of water reflect the light as they slide down the skin below her neck. She grins at Alyce.

'The video you saw probably illustrates the crux of my tale so far. That was when my uncle's story and mine diverged. Permanently. It's a beautifully shot movie, don't you think? You never see the face of the woman, and that adds to the tension, I reckon. But what you do see is how a man looks when he's both fucking and dying, when his semen is still pumping into you, even as his thick arterial blood is spurting out all over you.'

'Sandra, I can help you. Whatever it is that you've gone through...'

'Just shut up! Look, I don't feel like pulling you anymore. So, go on and drag yourself onto that great big book over there. And please don't take too long about it, or I'll start putting the knife in places where it's really going to hurt.'

The teacher slides her legs up, and pushes herself with her good arm onto her knees. The pain is like a spark to the powder of her fury.

'You're insane, Sandra! People are going to be looking for me! There are almost twenty witnesses who know that you

85

were with me.' Alyce is so angry that it's as if she is seeing herself from afar; a bruised and dishevelled woman spitting the words out like venom. But Sandra merely stares her down.

'Oh, my dear Alyce. It's all part of the tale. It could go anywhere from here. But whatever happens, people are going to know my story. It's not over, not by a long shot. There's still so much to come.'

Alyce hangs her head, fatigue taking over as quickly as anger had. She gets slowly to her feet, and walks across to the large book. Sandra jerks her knife upward, indicating for Alyce to climb on.

'Up near the bells.'

Alyce slowly steps up the inner spine of the book, her boots pressing into the firm rubber. She sits and tries to shift her fractured arm into a more comfortable position. Sandra is fiddling with the tripod-mounted digital SLR camera. The large knife rests on the table, readily accessible to the student. Alyce tries to slow her breathing, to calm her mind. During the past few minutes, a part of her brain has been subconsciously filtering a disjointed progression of possible plans and outcomes, without anything coalescing into something that might work. It is possible that, before the lights went out, Sandra was going to try and seduce her here on the book, before dispatching her in the same way she'd apparently done her uncle. If so, she might have hidden a weapon nearby. Alyce glances around quickly at the props, but it is almost certain that the knife Sandra might have used is the same as the one now resting on the table.

Alyce suddenly realises how quiet the room has become. Sometime in the last five minutes, the rain has stopped, or at least diminished to a soft, silent drizzle.

Sandra walks over to the computer. She plays around with the mouse until the sound of chanting begins to seep out of the laptop's speakers. Alyce guesses there are three or four kids' voices in unison singing the lyrics to the familiar old nursery rhyme:

Oranges and lemons, say the bells of St. Clement's,
You owe me five farthings, say the bells of St. Martin's...

Sandra pauses the song and grins at Alyce.

'When I was taking portraits of kids dressed up as various nursery rhyme characters, I began to realise there was something missing. Even though many of the verses had violent overtones, the children were just acting out a part; they weren't in any real danger. And there was no consideration towards the actual meaning behind so many of the rhymes. Who amongst them would have known, for example, that 'Jack and Jill' was probably a reference to King Louis XVI and Marie Antoinette of France, whose heads were very much in need of vinegar and brown paper after being separated from their bodies by the guillotine. Or that 'Oranges and Lemons' gleefully lists some of the major bells of London summoning condemned persons to their execution at Newgate Prison.'

Sandra clicks the mouse and the rhyme starts up again. The chanting children run through the rest of the verse until the end of 'I do not know, say the great bells of Bow', then go back to the start. Meanwhile, Sandra bends down at the candle, and strikes a match to light it. Alyce watches silently, waiting, and thinking.

'Life was cheap, wretched, and expendable, back when so many of those nursery rhymes were written,' says Sandra with sudden venom, 'and yet here were these privileged brats, sitting there, all dollied up while their parents cooed like infatuated doves. I wanted them to suffer. I wanted so badly to hurt them. And yet how could I? The kids belonged to someone. There would be questions, consequences...I tried to be nice, I really did, but still our client numbers began to dwindle.'

The chanting of the children coming through the laptop speakers has changed. It is getting louder, and the verse is now being sung as a round, but not in a coordinated fashion, so that the rhyme is garbled.

'A solution presented itself though,' continued Sandra, 'First, in the form of my uncle, and then through our fortuitous bonding at school, Alyce. I thought to myself, these were people that would hardly be missed. People with no partners, no family on the mountain. Willing subjects for my stories. Oh, make no mistake, my uncle resisted to the end. He wept with shame from the moment I seduced him. But by then it was too late, of course. And you, Alyce, were so easily manipulated. So now you're going to have the starring role in a re-enactment of my favourite nursery rhyme, all captured in glorious Full-HD video.'

Sandra presses a button on the digital SLR. Then she carefully picks up the burning candle in its holder and walks slowly towards the foot of the foam rubber book. The recorded chant of 'Oranges and Lemons' continues, jarring in its discordance. Then, layered under, a bell begins to toll, again and again, and suddenly the voices pitch in unison and begin to sing the last verse of the nursery rhyme.

Here comes a candle to light you to bed.

Sandra bends down and quickly sweeps something out from under where the giant book begins to rise up from the floor.

And here comes a chopper to chop off your head.

An axe gleams in Sandra's right hand, reflecting the light of the candle held in her left.

Chip, chop, chip, chop.

Sandra advances slowly up the foam rubber towards Alyce.

The last one's dead.

Alyce flings her good arm forward, her fingers curled around the spray bottle of Aeroguard that she'd slipped out of a pocket of her cargo pants. She presses down hard on the nozzle, directing a concentrated spray of the insect repellent towards the burning candle. There is a flash of ignition and the super-heated air rolls back over Sandra, who staggers back, dropping the axe and candle. Alyce shimmies between two foam bells and scrambles over the side of the book, hugging her broken arm to her stomach. Sandra lurches towards her, rubbing at her eyes. Alyce holds the Aeroguard bottle like a cosh, and swings hard at Sandra's head as she slips past her. She doesn't make full contact, but it's enough to rock the girl back. Light is intensifying like a second dawn through the half-closed door, and Alyce's shoes slap the floor as she heads straight towards it, sprinting as if trying to outrun the surging pain in her fractured arm. Then she is into the first studio, angling to the left to avoid the debris. Before her, the curtain in the doorway wavers, and a man steps through from the reception room. Light from an incipient sunbeam casts a messianic halo over his face.

'Looks like I got back here just in time,' says Richard Stratton. But he is looking past Alyce towards Sandra, who is emerging from the book room with axe in hand. As the girl moves to join Stratton, a shutter seems to open in Alyce's mind, and she suddenly sees again the video of Sandra seducing and murdering her uncle, and how its aspect is changing, as if someone is moving the camera around the room.

But it is not this that causes Alyce to fall to her knees, hope emptying from her heart as rapidly as the strength draining from her muscles. It is the large book that Stratton is holding in his hands, with an A3 size photograph of Alyce's face on the cover.

Sandra positions herself next to the male biology teacher, and they exchange a smile.

'Oh, Alyce. I have a confession to make,' says Sandra. 'I've been unfaithful. I've strayed from the straight and the narrow. May the devil take my soul…Oh! He already has.' She smiles again at Stratton.

'A lunatic after my own heart.' He grins. 'Did you know we both share an interest in embalming, amongst other things? I think young Sandra here has a hankering to be a mortician.'

'As long as I can still tell stories,' says Sandra. 'There are so many tales that can be derived from a person's passing over from life to death.'

'Speaking of which, haven't we got something special lined up for you, Alyce. Sandra, a hand please...'

Stratton and Sandra each take hold of a cover of the book. Then, as Alyce watches ashen-faced, they slowly part the pages towards the centre to reveal the shallow cavity.

The book is empty, and waiting to tell Alyce's story.

Creep's Motel
Jeremy Hayes

The rain was coming down with a vengeance. The windshield wipers were barely able to keep up, making visibility nearly non-existent. Gordon could see very little of the road ahead and his wife was now in a state of panic.

'You can't even see the road. I think we need to stop.'

'Stop where, Martha? I can't just stop. This is a highway. You want some truck to come up from behind and run right over us?'

'Well, pull off the road at least. I didn't mean for you to stop right here in the middle.'

Their weekend trip from the Big City to Shallow Lake had gone horribly awry. What should have only been a two-hour drive was now four, and they felt they were no closer to their destination than they had been two hours earlier.

'I told you that road didn't look right back there. You should have kept going straight.'

'The directions said to make a left off Highway Nine.'

'Yes, but it said to make a left onto Kingsway. That road you took didn't say Kingsway and I think that turn came a lot sooner than it should have.'

'I was told the first left was Kingsway. Perhaps the wind blew the sign down. That should have been the correct turn.'

'Obviously, it wasn't.'

Thunder cracked overhead and it was so loud that Gordon nearly veered right off the road. Martha shrieked.

'We really need to stop somewhere,' she implored. 'Where do you think we are?'

'I haven't seen a sign in hours. I was thinking we should be near Bridgeway Township, but none of this looks familiar to me.'

'I haven't even seen a street light or a gas bar in over an hour. Please, we need to stop at the next one we see.'

'I'll gladly stop at the next gas bar. We're going to run out of fuel if we don't find one soon.'

Martha's face turned even paler. 'Oh, Gordon, why didn't you fill up before we left?'

'It should have only been a two-hour drive. We had enough for that. Look, there is another road up here on the left.'

'Can you see a sign? What road is it?'

'I can't see a sign at all. I think we should take it, though.'

'No, Gordon, no more side roads. Let's just stay on the highway.'

'But maybe we could find some houses and ask someone where we are.'

'It's almost midnight. You think we're just going to go knock on some stranger's door in this kind of weather? Who in their right mind would answer? Just stay on this road and we're bound to come across something soon.'

'Fine.'

Gordon gripped the steering wheel so tightly his knuckles were white. He had never driven in such a storm before. Lightning arced across the sky and momentarily lit up the road ahead as if it were the middle of day. Both their hearts sank at the sight before them.

'Did you see that, Martha? The bridge is completely flooded.'

Martha sighed. 'I suppose we will have to go back to that last turnoff then.'

'Maybe if I get a good run at it we can make it across the bridge.'

Martha was mortified. 'You will do no such thing! Turn around.'

'Fine.'

Gordon doubled back and turned down the nameless side

road. They were in a heavily wooded area which made everything appear that much darker. The road was not paved and his new worry was getting stuck in the mud, though he didn't dare voice that concern. Martha was already in such a frenzy that one more provocation would send her completely over the edge. He also thought it best not to mention that the needle on the fuel indicator was now in the red.

Twenty minutes later, the woods thinned and the road came to an intersection. Gordon and Martha both smiled and allowed themselves a moment to laugh at their sudden good fortune. They spotted a motel on the other side of the intersection. Its neon vacancy sign was on, but two letters weren't working. To put the couple in an even better mood, there was a gas pump at the motel.

'Someone is looking out for us,' Martha said jubilantly.

Gordon breathed a sigh of relief. The timing couldn't have been better. He entered the empty parking lot and another flash of lightning lit up the night sky.

'Oh, good heavens,' Martha said. 'Did you see the sign?'

Gordon had. 'Creep's Motel? Who would name a motel that?'

'I don't see any other cars here. Strange for a Friday night.'

Gordon was just thinking the same thing.

The motel was in a terrible state. To suggest it would need some fixing up would be an understatement. It was a long, single-level building with what appeared to be ten rooms and a main office. The only visible light came from within the office.

Gordon parked in front of the first room, adjacent to the office. His headlights revealed a broken window and a door that didn't sit properly on its hinges.

Worry crept back into Martha's mind. 'Ah, I don't think I like the look of this place. They certainly named it well, because it gives me the creeps.'

'Don't be so silly. A lot of the old motels out in the middle of nowhere are like this. The storm is just making it appear creepier than it really is.'

'I don't know. I think it would look just as creepy in the middle of the day. How about you just get some gas and find out where we are, then we can leave.'

'Martha, I'm exhausted and this storm is horrendous. We're going to need to wait somewhere for it to clear up.'

'Not here.'

'Nonsense. A place like this will probably cost next to nothing for a room. I can see someone in the office. Are you coming in with me?'

Martha nodded reluctantly. She had no real desire to get out of the car, but they'd been driving so long she figured she should at least use the restroom.

The pair ran the short distance from their car to the office but still arrived inside soaking wet. It was as if they'd both just jumped fully-clothed into a pool.

Chimes jingled on the door and startled the middle-aged man who had been asleep behind the front counter.

'Oh my, where did you folk come from?' he asked, rubbing his eyes.

'That's a long story, my friend. First, we need to know where we are,' Gordon replied.

'The middle of nowhere,' the man joked.

Gordon wasn't in the mood. 'We're from the Big City and we're trying to get to Shallow Lake. How far are we from the lake?'

'Shallow Lake? Hmm,' he scratched his chin in thought. 'I don't reckon I have ever heard of Shallow Lake.'

'Never heard of…oh, never mind. What town are we in?'

'Oldhill.'

'Oldhill? I have no idea where Oldhill is. How far away are we from the Big City?'

'Oh, I would say purdy far.'

Gordon was finding it difficult to keep his eyes off the man's stained shirt. He was grubby, and his office was in disarray. Layers of dust lined every surface. Perhaps Martha was right.

'Look, maybe we could just get some gas and a map, and then we'll be on our way?'

'Our pump is empty.'

'What?'

'Hasn't been used in years.'

Gordon noticed his wife tense up as she realised they weren't going to be going anywhere anytime soon.

'Joe? Who are ya talking to?' a woman said, as she entered the office from a back room. 'Oh, howdy folks.'

The woman's hair was dishevelled and she was removing the remnants of her supper from her teeth with a toothpick.

'This is my wife, Maude. Maude, these folk just arrived from that wicked storm.'

'Ah, be needin a room, will ya?'

'Well, we were just hoping to get some gas and directions and be on our way.'

'Our pump is empty.'

'Yeah, we just heard that grim news.'

'So, ya best be bringin yer bags in. Ya got the pick of any room ya like. The storm should clear come mornin, don't ya be thinkin, Joe?'

'I reckon so, Maude.'

'Got some leftovers in the back room here that's still warm. Once ya get settled, I can bring some to yer room.'

Martha blanched. She couldn't imagine the state of the kitchen in this place.

'That won't be necessary. We had a big dinner before we left and had some snacks in the car.'

'Suit yerself.'

'Since you are kinda in a jam, with the storm and all, I'll even offer you our best room for the regular price.' Joe smiled.

'Ah, much appreciated. I suppose I'll go grab our bags from the car.'

Martha grabbed Gordon's arm. 'I am coming with you, I, ah, forgot something.'

'Nonsense, Junior can fetch your bags. Maude, go wake Junior.'

'Oh, no, no. No need to wake anyone,' Gordon insisted.

Before heading back out into the rain, Gordon turned, with a burning question on his mind.

'Just curious, what's with the name of your place? Creep's Motel? Really? Are you trying to keep people away?'

Both Joe and Maude bristled at the comment. 'Well, that's our name is all. We're Joe and Maude Creep.'

Martha pinched Gordon's arm to the point where it hurt and then dragged him out the front door. The rain hadn't let up one bit, so they both ran as fast as they could back to the car. Once inside, Martha whirled on her husband.

'As if the Creeps weren't creepy enough, you had to go and insult them!'

'How could I know that was their name? Who has the name, Creep?'

'They do!'

'Suits them too.'

'We're not staying here.'

'What? We have no choice.'

'I can't sleep in this place. I have a very bad feeling. They give me the heebie jeebies.'

'Well, we have no gas and no idea where we are. Not to mention this storm.'

'Didn't you say once that you drove a half hour with the gas needle on red?'

'Yes, but we've already been driving with it in the red. We won't get very far.'

'I don't care. Anywhere is better than here.'

'You say that now, but you'll change your mind when we're sleeping in the car out on some dark road somewhere.'

'No, I won't.'

'Dear, be reasonable. It's not safe for us out there. Now, we have to stay here tonight and then we can assess things in the morning. Hopefully, the storm will stop by then. We found this place, so I'm sure there's somewhere else close by where we can get gas, but we can't just go driving blindly in the dark.'

'My gut tells me something is off about this place.'

'Don't be silly. It's dark, it's stormy, and the owners are a touch creepy. You're letting your imagination run wild.'

Martha screamed at the top of her lungs, which caused Gordon to shriek as well, though he wasn't quite sure why. His wife had been looking past him, so he turned and shrieked a second time at the sight of a face pressed against the car window.

'I got the key to your room,' Joe said, from within the hood of his raincoat. 'It's right over here if you want to follow me with your bags.'

It took a while for the couple to get their breathing back under control. Martha gave her husband a glare that told him she didn't want to get out of the car.

'Come on. It will only be a few more hours until morning. We'll leave as soon as dawn breaks. I'll grab the bags from the trunk. Let's go.'

Gordon grabbed three bags and they both ran for the cover of the motel's awning, then followed Joe down to room 105. Gordon was pleased that at least this room's window was intact and the door sat properly on its hinges.

Joe unlocked the door and invited the couple to follow him inside. The room was quite dark, so the couple hesitated by the doorway until their escort had entered and turned on a small lamp next to the double bed.

Their best room? Gordon and Martha thought silently in unison.

'Is there anything else you need?' their host asked.

'I think we'll be fine, thanks,' Gordon answered.

'Once you get settled, you can drop by the office and get

things squared away. We accept cash and charge cards.'

Gordon nodded and closed the door quickly behind Joe Creep. He turned back and surveyed the room again. Dust covered every surface within the small room and the awful wallpaper was peeling in several places. There was one double bed, a side table with the lamp, and a writing desk under the window, next to the front door. A tiny bathroom was located at the back of the room and there was a connecting door linking the room with its left-hand neighbour. A horrible painting of a family standing in front of a farm hung crookedly on one of the walls. It looked like a child had painted it with his fingers.

Martha inspected the bed and wrinkled her nose in disgust. 'The sheets are all stained. I can't stay here.'

'We have no choice. We can sleep on the floor if you prefer. We can pretend we're camping.'

Martha was in no mood for jokes.

'I'm going to go pay while you get comfortable.'

Thunder cracked and Martha jumped in fright. 'Don't leave me in this room alone.'

'I'll just be a minute. Lock the door behind me if you like. And stop worrying.'

Gordon left and Martha did indeed lock the deadbolt. Her heart was racing a million miles a minute. She hadn't been exaggerating in the least when she'd said her gut told her something was off about the place. It was just a nagging feeling that wouldn't let up or allow her to relax.

She walked about the room, conducting a thorough inspection. Even the carpet was stained, she noticed with disgust. She stopped in front of the ugly painting and something odd immediately drew her attention. Three people stood in front of a farm, and one of them had a hole for an eye. There was an actual hole through the painting. Curious, Martha pulled the painting off the wall, and her stomach turned upon discovering a small round hole in the wall. The perfect peephole, she figured, from the room next-door.

She quickly retrieved a tissue from her purse and stuffed it into the dark hole. Goose bumps ran up and down her arms and neck. She then glanced at the connecting door, and her heart skipped a beat. There was no lock. She carefully tried the doorknob and found that the door was indeed locked, but from the other side.

A knock on the front door nearly had Martha jumping straight through the roof of the room. Once she recovered, she quickly unlocked the door and pulled it open.

'Gordon, I nearly…' Martha's sentence was interrupted by another scream.

It wasn't Gordon, but a huge hulk whose face was concealed behind the hood of a raincoat.

'W-who are y-you?' she managed to ask.

No answer.

'My husband will be b-back any m-moment now.'

No answer.

'P-please don't h-hurt me.'

'Junior! You get away from there now. Stop scaring the nice lady!' Joe shouted from outside.

Martha breathed a giant sigh of relief when he walked away without a word.

Gordon arrived, accompanied by Joe. 'I apologise, ma'am. Junior was just curious to see the new guests is all.'

'He doesn't say much, does he?'

'Junior's a simple lad. Well, goodnight, folks. Give a holler if you need anything.'

Once the door was closed again, Gordon noticed the look on Martha's face.

'I'm not staying here,' she stated, a quiver in her voice.

'What? I just paid.'

'We're leaving.'

'The man apologised for his son. He didn't mean to scare you. You heard him, he's just simple.'

'It's not just that, Gordon. Come here. I found a peephole in the wall. It was concealed by the painting.'

'You're jumping to conclusions.'

'Am I? What about this door that connects to the next room? It's only locked from the other side. Anyone could come in here from the other room.'

'Oh, stop it. Come in here for what purpose?'

'To murder us in our sleep!'

'Do you realise how ridiculous you sound? You watch too many of those late-night movies.'

'Something doesn't feel right. These Creeps are *real* creeps.'

'It's just their name! You're letting this storm affect your judgement. This is all in your mind. Granted, the room could be a little better, but...'

'A little better?'

'Fine. The room is a dump. The whole place is a dump. But we are stuck here, just for tonight.'

'I refuse to stay here. We're leaving.'

'But, dear! We won't get far before we run out of gas!'

'We'll be away from here and that's all that matters.'

'Oh, for Pete's sake!'

#

Maude rushed into the main office and the sound of her shuffling slippers jolted Joe awake. He'd only just nodded off behind the counter again.

'I thought I heard something,' she said. 'Joe, that young couple just drove off.'

'Eh?'

'That couple. They just left.'

Joe joined his wife by the front window and caught a glimpse of tail lights before they faded from view.

'Hmm, you're right.'

'Dang it! I bet Junior plum scared them off. I told ya that ya

100

shoulda hit that one in the head with the shovel when he was in here payin.'

'Now, Maude, you know I prefer to get them in their sleep.'

'Maybe we ought to send Junior after them? They might not get far with little gas.'

'We don't want Junior catchin a cold. It's miserable out there.'

'Well, there ain't much left from that last couple. Ya want us to starve?'

'Don't forget we still have that travellin salesman in the cold storage.'

Maude grunted to herself and shuffled away, while Joe, glancing out into the darkness, shrugged his shoulders, then resumed his place behind the counter, where he soon nodded off again.

And Then There Were Two
Pym Schaare

As she lay back on the bed, the storm outside was resolute in its mission to frighten the fragile. It wasn't Amber who was the fearful one, but Adam, her soon to be ex, as he lay quietly with her feet working his penis. And it was annoying her. But not for long. She was resolving the issue. When he began to come, she smiled as she reached to palm the little pearl inlay gun from under the pillow. Bringing her hand up, she took the shot at his head. She hoped his cries and final grunt blended with the ferocity of the thunder and lightning. For what seemed like the smallest of moments, when she was thrown back hard against the headboard, lightning-like bolts made their way through every cell in her body. Her eyes, for a split second, widened in fear, freezing her smile. It took another second for her lips to soften back across her teeth, a dimple forming.

Letting herself relax, she closed her eyes against the stress that had widened them a minute ago, and reflected on what had transpired earlier at dinner, when the storm had barrelled its way toward them. In its absolute wisdom, the storm had offered Amber another option for ridding herself of the ever-clingier Adam. Now she found it irritated her to be cossetted at every opportunity in the name of love. At the beginning, she'd enjoyed the attention, but now she felt smothered by it.

#

Her phone call to work two days ago to call in her accumulated two and half days had made her sweat. The beads of moisture that had collected on her forehead had run all the way down to her mouth. Her salty request to her coordinator felt uneasy for a few seconds. And messy. When she wiped her mouth, with the tissue from the nearby box, she calmed: the fragility left her. And she was again reminded that calm was her normal. Frazzled was not.

Completing her request for leave over the phone gave Amber sufficient time to upload the street map where her rendezvous with Adam would be masterminded. There were moments in the conversation where what her boss was saying barely registered, but she eventually got it sorted.

As she continued to stalk the map on the screen, embedding its streetscape in her mind to make sure she knew the surrounding area in case something went awry with her plan, she finally settled.

Amber called Adam. The short reminder about where they were meeting for their designated role-play was quickly relayed over the second mobile she owned. It was something they had been doing over the past six months, to spice things up. This time, the game was to pick her up outside the library three hours away. As he rolled the window down, the setup was to call her Sissie, short for Cassandra, and nothing at all to do with Amber.

He replied knowingly, nodding agreement, 'Okay, can't wait.'

Amber's early morning attention was hijacked by thoughts of the new life she was embarking on, and knowing that money would be no object sweetened the dream. Smiling to herself, she could already feel the fullness of her future freedom.

With the first rays of the day's sun following her, she strode into her bedroom and inspected her red bikini, matching sarong, and new Jimmy Choo shoes, while contemplating the space left in her bag. Even with her toiletries, the bag wouldn't be too heavy to carry the few blocks from where she would leave her car.

Her intention to run away fit the role well. Her anxiety, for all intents and purposes, would suit the act. Gazing into the art deco mirror, the face in it shot her a strange look. She saw the doubt there in that moment. But only for a second. As her mood swung back into top gear, she gave the brocade bedspread the once-over, and picked up the bag.

She shook her head free and headed for the car, but busy images kept darting across her mind, so she slid the bag onto the back seat and opened it for a last minute check, slipping her hand down the sides, where she felt her underwear. Satisfied, she zipped the bag closed, stepped back, and slammed the door.

Finally satisfied with her choices, her mind sang with the tune of a slow love song; the kind you danced to without looking up. And it was that slow dance in her mind that brought her attention to her wrist slung over the shoulder of a partner, one that embodied an array of dreams of love. It was a magnificently bejewelled wrist.

With the engine already rumbling, it was a startled hand that turned the key again, cutting the motor. She reached back to the rear passenger seat, fingers searching again. After a speedy feel around the jewellery purse, she rolled the satin edges together, tying the whole lot down with the red satin ribbon. Done. She zipped it shut, the sharp sound prickling like lightning.

Ready to set off, she was interrupted by the running buzz from the green arrow on her phone. She nearly jumped out of her skin when her work number appeared. Quickly swiping left to right, she uttered, 'Yes, it's Amber.'

Nerrida, her HR coordinator, had rung to confirm the details of her leave. There had been a miscommunication.

'Sorry about that. Yes, that's right. It does rather seem as if we are both a bit lost when it comes to dates.' Laughing it off, hoping the double-entendre sounded half polite. 'I've been at it twenty-four seven.'

The friendly reply seemed to settle the confusion. 'Yeah, we all need a break sometimes'.

'We sure do,' she said, her teeth bared, relieved her frustration was hidden.

'Have a good time. Don't do anything I wouldn't do, or if you do, do it badder and better.' Nerrida giggled.

Despite having settled that, Amber couldn't help but feel uneasy and wondered whether she had forgotten something other than her calendar dates.

After hanging up, she reached over to the back seat yet again. She had to find what was niggling at her. She checked her satin jewellery purse and realised what was wrong. She'd forgotten something so very important.

Leaping from the car, she dashed back to her bedroom. It was on top of her wardrobe, where she kept her winter jumpers. She reached up and sought out the bronze case, then sat on the bed and carefully flicked the satin holds aside. She took the piece in her hand. The fit was perfect. She made a fist around it, palming the gun out of sight.

A nod and smile to no one in particular warmed her belly at the sheer art of it. Making a quick retreat out the front door, past the many faceted reflections of herself, Amber's haste nearly landed her in the garden when her silver stiletto hit a loose paving stone. She steadied herself, continuing her race to the car, before a neighbour caught sight of her. She didn't need any gossip to follow her.

Any latent fear or anxiety that had left her sweaty in the hidden crevasses of her body settled as soon as she steered the car out of the drive. By the time she'd parked under a tree two blocks away from the library, she was already three hours from home. Nobody knew her here. And she was glad.

Stepping from the car, she opened the back door to reach for her overnight bag. *Check*, she thought to herself. *Car parked, and locked. Check.*

Bag in hand, she walked over to the concrete path leading to the library, happy to avoid getting her heels stuck in the thick grass or caked with mud.

The huge trees that flanked the library must have been at least a hundred years old, and the wooden benches underneath them gave her a perfect view while she waited for Adam.

From her vantage point at the high end of the wooden bench, Amber watched traffic slide past. A half-hour later, the sight of Adam in his hire car, turning off the highway and onto the service road, made her heart miss a beat. It would be another few minutes before he was idling alongside of her, to give her the once-over.

'Sissie,' she whispered, as she looked in through the car window.

'Adam, I'm Adam,' he said, not having thought of a moniker. He opened the door slowly, and he watched her long legs make a V shape as she settled in bedside him. Pulling the car door shut, she leaned back to place her bag on the back seat. She gave him a dimpled smile, and he reached over, playing his fingers down the side of her face.

Where they were to dine was another two hours away, and it was to the saucy sounds of his favourite jazz that Adam drove. This was a night of celebration, with a morning at the beach to follow if tomorrow was as sunny. Nodding to the beat of the music, all seemed calm in the car. Until a newsflash cut in and they heard the storm warning; it was going to be a bad one. Amber's heart pounded and she closed her mouth to stop herself from gasping.

When they finally swung into the car park of the restaurant, Amber's earlier dark mood subsided. Inside the restaurant, they were ushered in as Mr. and Mrs. Fury, a choice made by Adam. Mrs. Fury smiled at the waiter, as he waved a white damask napkin across her lap. In no time, she was holding a long stemmed glass of Perrier. Amber felt the high-end glamour of faux French gold-trimmed mirrors gave her an emotional edge that would render well with her later plans. Seeing herself from every angle gave her an update of the beauty of it all.

With her mood smoothed over by the Latin groove playing in the background, Amber rolled and shimmied her shoulders at Adam. She was bewitching in her role, and Adam lapped up

106

every second of it. They must surely have appeared to be madly in love to the other diners.

The thought of missing out on her bikini beach day tomorrow charged her face with worry, but to Adam, the flames burning bright on her cheeks looked like the reflection of his desire. Her plans would have to be changed, which was bothersome, but the end result would be the same. She would come back from the secluded bay on her own.

The bay she had chosen off the Great Ocean Road had been one of many locations for photo shoots she had done in the past. Knowledge of the more secluded locations came from her modelling days. In those days, nude photography had to be kept out of the public eye, even if the photos did eventually turn up in magazines. She thought many a time about the double standards of the business. She'd moved away from those days. She was the smart one out of the many girls who had since faded out of the limelight and away from the money.

Amber had chosen study: economics and accounting. They were her poison. And she did them well. Passing with flying colours. The finance company that had snatched her up had never looked back; nor had she. She had made them a lot of money, and vice versa. Her mind floated with past images of herself. As she swirled her drink, her lazy second, in her long fingered hand, she was interrupted, 'Hey, Amb...Sissie,' he corrected himself, 'back to earth...you're aeons away'.

'Sorry, it's just so lovely here, with you. I guess I got carried away by all this,' she added, with a flourish of her hand which included him in the gorgeous décor.

Taking advantage of the moment, Adam leaned his long frame across Amber. The deep kiss gentled her back to reality.

Once they had resumed their seats, the waiter arrived with their entrées, which were promptly followed by their eagerly awaited main course. Neither had eaten lunch that day, but that wasn't the only thing that left Amber feeling starved.

She was enjoying her medium rare fillet mignon when an

107

almighty clap of thunder landed in the middle of their reverie over the meal and startled her.

The waiter tried to bring them up to speed on the weather.

'In these regions, you never know when the storm is hours, a day, two days, or even minutes away. Forecasters get it wrong most of the time. I hope it won't spoil your plans. We do have suites upstairs, just in case'.

Amber responded quickly and sweetly before Adam could.

'No, that's okay. We have family close by. But thanks anyway.' Her smile sealed the lie.

Cutting into her mignon, Amber felt her veins freeze at the sight of the pink meat in front of her. She shuddered as she withdrew her bloodied knife. She had always liked her steak rare and was surprised by her reaction.

For a moment, she found herself caught up with what lay ahead. And with that thought, she wasn't sure what had frightened her most; that she could go through with it, or the opposite. Laying the knife down at the side of her plate, she contemplated the reflection she caught in one of the many mirrors surrounding her. She had to keep a smile on her face. She didn't want Adam to see her without one.

'Mmmm, this is orgasmic,' she purred, and her tongue slowly worked the next mouthful of mignon. She felt the juices swish around, and all the while, she reassembled her plans. By the time she had finished the third bite, along with the seared vegetables they were both sharing, her inner turmoil had subsided. In that short time, Amber's plan had been reassigned to another location, one they had to find tonight after dinner. Even though they were more than three hundred kilometres from their respective homes in the greater area of Melbourne, Amber scanned the restaurant to make sure there was no one there she knew.

All good. Tick.

She liked ticking things off. It made it real, and gave any project she was on an air of success. It made her feel calm, confident that it would all work out.

Rising to leave, Adam was still fanning down the waiter's effusive invitation to stay in one of the suites. It pleased Amber that he had followed her earlier lead on the invitation and declined. She didn't have to come across as the tough one. This way was easier. There was less to remember them by, apart from the pass on the suite.

Adam did all he could to keep Sissie dry as they ran to the car. He held his jacket over her head, but it was futile against the sheet of cold rain.

By the time he had closed the door, she was already reaching for the towel in the back. She dried herself with one end of it and left the other for Adam.

One look at each other and all they could do was laugh. They were like drowned rats.

When Adam's face and hands were dry, they made for the motel sign Amber had spotted fleetingly through the lightning blaze. The spark which had cut the sky into so many different parts had revealed a B&B beside the motel. Driving carefully, Adam idled into the drive, stopping under the awning in front of the small reception sign.

He returned with the keys to room twelve. 'Two nights.'

'Ooh, okay. Sounds good. That'll fit with my leave,' she said with a wink, not mentioning the extra day.

For a fraction of a second, his smile pulled her heartstrings. Another look at him and she would start to shy away from her plan. If she continued to warm to his love for her, she would be done. But she quickly turned her thoughts to the darker part of her heart, the part that was tired of him. And it worked. It strengthened her resolve to go through with everything she had been planning for the last two weeks.

They found number twelve, a surprisingly large suite around the back, where the garden of the B&B was, and parked the car in its designated space. Adam got out, opened the door, and dropped his bag on the floor as he rushed to the bathroom to

109

get a dry towel. He then hurried back and held the towel over Amber as she walked into the room.

Once inside, he headed back into the bathroom. Amber knew he was frozen right through.

'I'll unpack.'

She smiled at him as his clothes slid from his body. Chilled to the bone, Adam couldn't wait to get under the hot shower.

'I won't be too long. Maybe a bit longer than usual though.'

He shivered.

She smiled at him, then repeated, 'I'll unpack.'

She hoped the sound of metal zippers, wardrobe doors stopping at a hard jolt, and thumping on shelves would make it sound like she was unpacking. She knew he wouldn't be looking in there. He always unpacked the following morning. She couldn't stand it, feeling it was a disorganised way to be. But right now, it was the right kind of disorganised.

His longer than usual shower worked, giving her time to stash the little pearl gun, put her mobile on the bedside table next to the obligatory bible, and leave her watch. But the bible made her shudder, so she shoved it into the drawer. She'd had enough judgement in the past. Banging the drawer shut provided some redemption.

Once Adam had finished, she laid her wet clothes over the chaise and made for the shower. As she passed him, she purred and puckered her lips. The kiss was quick but soft.

From under the shower, she heard Adam pull the bed sheets back and fluff the pillows. She nearly died on the spot.

She held her breath, but he didn't utter a word, so she knew he hadn't touched hers. She waited another second before putting the shower on full-bore. The hard stream of water somehow took away the fright she'd just had.

Dry and warm, she let the thick fluffy towel fall onto the bathmat. Picking up her lingerie, she drew the hot pink crotchless knickers over her tanned body. When she added the red and gold bustier, it made her glow. With the robe over the top, the surprise would be all his eventually. It had been ages since they'd had this kind of fun. She simply had to make the most of it.

She steeled herself and entered the bedroom, but there was no hiding her shock. Adam was a sight to behold. He'd chosen to dress gangsta style. He laughed as he unzipped his costume, and as it fell around his ankles, he extricated a gun from its holster and waved it high above his head. It made her heart skip a beat, and she felt sick for a second.

'Sissie, it's a fake. But a good one, huh?'

Amber collected herself and climbed onto the bed. Undoing her robe, she bent her legs, letting them fall apart, wide, one at a time. She found his arousal beautiful.

He pulled her up, into a deep kiss, and she pulled him into a twist beneath her. Once he was under her, she slid herself over him, whole. Taking him inside her excited and panicked her at the same time.

He didn't seem to notice, which made Amber reflect on how making love or having outrageous sex could sound just about like any emotion possible, even anger and fear. She knew he would soon be spent inside her, so took her pleasure just as quickly, gasping in chorus with him.

As they rolled away from each other, panting, Amber's mind was already busy trying to figure out how to get him into the desired position for her plan to work. Within minutes, the problem solved itself. Adam slid to the end of the bed, his feet at her lips and her feet at his.

She gently cricked her legs so her feet could take his penis between them. Her heart raced as she manipulated the slide and rotation, knowing he would rise again. His semen spilled all over her feet, trickling over each toe at a time.

When the gun went off, it was unexpectedly quiet. His eyes bore witness to his shock for an instant, and when he stilled, the noise hung in the room, the memory of it frightening her.

She looked away from the sight of him at the end of the bed, then picked the mobile up and fingered the redial button.

'Yes, come straight away. The door is open, so close it when you arrive.'

Three hours later, she heard the doorknob squeak, and her husband stepped inside. She saw the alarm on his face at the sight of the man at the end of the bed. His head was moving back and forth at the gruesome sight, as if he were at a tennis match. It was unlike any other movement she had ever seen him make; his head seemed to rotate, and if he didn't stop soon, she was sure there was every chance of it falling from his neck and shoulders and onto the floor. Clunk.

'See, Peter, I do love you,' was meant as an assurance.

But the shock remained on his face as he uttered but never quite completed his response. 'I always knew you loved meee...'

She watched as he slumped to the ground like an accordion, folding and unfolding, resurrecting to full height, then down again. It continued for at least twenty seconds and was freaking her out, while at the same time, there was something awkwardly funny about it.

The storm outside claimed her as the window latches shuddered, just like her heart. Lightning bolts and roars of thunder hammered her every nerve, judging her.

With the suite at the back of the building, she hoped all the noise had been contained. In any case, with wild weather rolling on in and inflicting all the fierceness nature had to offer, there was no getting away. She would have to remain there for the rest of the night to shelter from the storm.

In the calm of the morning, she quickly gathered her things, not once looking at the two men. But they came at her from the large gilt mirrors, blurring themselves into a grotesque masterpiece of expressionistic art. In fright, she wrenched the door open, and doing her best to quell her fear, she made for the car; her car, the one Peter had driven across the Great Ocean Road to be with her. She unlocked the door, slid the bag onto the passenger seat, and drove away, never once looking back.

The Inimitable Livers
Mark McAuliffe

Chris managed to breathe easy. He was standing, wanted to stay standing, but he'd been pacing back and forth, looking jumpy, so he forced himself to stop, to stand still, dammit! His mouth was dry, but hell no, he didn't want a drink.

He felt panic. It ate at him. His chest felt tight and there was a hot taste of metal at the base of his tongue.

They were in Dominic's spacious living room. The fireplace had been neglected, so despite his heavy anorak, Chris was cold. Pale light came from only a few scattered lamps intruding vaguely from the fringes. It made long shadows and ominous black spots.

Even though Chris had been here several times, he felt slightly disorientated. The dark gave the artwork on the walls a haunting quality. Pale, stern faces with piercing eyes and judgemental expressions. The expensive ornamentation placed casually about took on strange proportions, monstrous forms.

The two girls sat on the over-stuffed sofa. The brunette, Kerri, looked more like she was perched there; alert, attentive, almost expectant, like she might launch herself at any moment. Eighteen, maybe, but probably closer to the wrong side of seventeen, Chris supposed. He'd seen her about Dominic's property many times. Very attractive, but hers was a classic beauty. Cold. It was the sort you might find carved in marble, or reproduced in fresco on a crumbling wall in Pompeii. He'd mentioned that once, in a casual conversation with Dominic.

'Oh yes, completely agree,' the octogenarian had replied. 'Indeed, one could imagine her as Agrippina, watching calmly on as Halotus fed Claudius the poison mushrooms, yes?'

Then one of those rumbling, throaty laughs of his. And

Chris, right at that moment, had wanted to ask just why he kept her, and the blonde, and the handful of others, hanging around? Was it solely to work on his market garden?

But he'd bitten his tongue, reflected that he really didn't need – or want – to know.

The skinny blonde (Terri? Tricia? Tina! Yes!) was rugged up and huddled behind the more dominant girl, as if trying to hide. She was a flighty little bird. Say boo and she'd squeak. Chris guessed she was even younger than Kerri. Right now he discounted her. She was the least distraction, not at all the danger.

But Bradley.

Oh, hell.

He must have emerged from the kitchen, and was regarding Chris from across the room. Those black, pinprick eyes of his, that twisted sneer he seemed to perpetually wear. Greasy hair combed back from a high forehead that was a red riot of acne. The same angry rash on his cheeks. The turtleneck he wore looked itchy. It didn't manage to conceal his blocky build. Dominic had told Chris that he hired him, on and off, as a handyman of sorts. Chris had no doubt just how handy he could be. He'd already noticed a cruel streak to the little bastard, the way he would bully some of the other young guys that Dominic had around to work on his garden. And the way he could have the two girls scurrying about with nothing more than a stern look.

Sweet Christ...

Chris had already considered his chances. If anything kicked off, his only real hope lay in flight, definitely not fight. Chris' tall, lanky body wasn't built for the fray. He was quick when he had to be, but would he be quick enough to make it to the back door? That's where he'd entered the house, and where he'd left his bike, as well as his wellies, just beneath the awning, to keep them out of the rain.

He might try the front door, which was closer. But

supposing it was locked? Even if it wasn't, he would need to run all the way home, but in this weather? He still had his socks on. They were thick, but he doubted they would spare his feet from some of the harsher terrain out there.

Come on! Think of something!

Chris looked from face to face. His fixed smile hurt. He could, of course, just say time was getting on, and he needed to be on his way, but then, it was the rain that had brought him here in the first place. He spared a quick glance out the window. Damn. It was still pelting out there.

Trapped!

An uncomfortable silence had descended. Probably only a handful of seconds, it felt much longer. Chris struggled to find something to say. He had nothing. Kerri leaned out even further. The blonde just kept staring. Those wet, puppy eyes.

It was Bradley who broke the silence.

'So,' he said, 'you won't have a drink? You're sure? I'm having one.'

'No,' Chris said, 'I'm sure...but thank you.'

Bradley stood by the drinks cabinet. He didn't make a move. His smirk stitched his lower face harder.

'Tina,' he said, 'um...scotch I think. Two fingers. Soda, no ice.'

The blonde cringed when she heard her name. She tried to huddle more into herself. Kerri poked her hard in the ribs. That got her motivated, got her scuttling. She was flustered. Glasses and bottles clinked and clacked. The measure of scotch that she poured was too much. She added just a splash of soda. It made Bradley grimace when he took a hefty swallow. He tried to hide the look on his face. Failed. He announced a satisfied, breathy sound.

'That's good,' he said. His voice sounded raw. 'Old Dom didn't – uh – doesn't penny pinch when it comes to his booze.'

Chris caught the slip, felt his gut clench.

'Um,' he managed, 'ah...y-you don't have to tell me...ha

116

ha…ah, yes, he's certainly the connoisseur…'

That was true enough. Many a Wednesday or Thursday night, over the last year or so, in this room, or more usually in Dominic's extensive library. Ever generous with his scotch and his brandy. And yes, Chris could have really done with one about now. But…

'I could go a Midori,' Kerri said. 'There's still some left, isn't there? In the fridge? Tina?'

The blonde scampered dutifully.

'Midori,' Bradley said. 'Fuckin' lolly water.'

He rolled his eyes at Chris, as if to say, *Women! Huh?*

Bright lightning briefly lit the room, followed almost immediately by splitting thunder. It made Chris flinch. Bradley finished his drink quickly and turned to fix himself another. Chris looked briefly at Kerri, who still had him in her eagle eyes, so he blinked away, scanned the dim walls instead. He focused on one of Dominic's favourite paintings in the room. Well, it was a print really (I may be rich, dear boy, but not *that* rich!), tucked away, deep in gloom. Memory provided detail.

The Death of Socrates. Jacques Louis David.

Often, dear boy, I just like to stand and contemplate…

The scene depicted the great Sage, defiant to the last.

Accused of corrupting the youth! Damn fools! Such petty minds…

The print depicted him surrounded by others, one young man, holding the poisoned chalice, looking away. Another youth, clutching his thigh. Supplication or worship?

Could he be Dominic's ideal role-model? Really? Chris had often detected a more…louche, cavalier streak…

Bradley suddenly brought him back to the moment.

'Shit! This is fuckin' great scotch. You really sure?'

Chris didn't answer. There was another painting, nearer to him. As lightning flashed, he caught a glimpse. *The Last Words of Marcus Aurelius* by Eugene Delacroix. Another of Dominic's great men, about to breathe his last. Surrounded by

117

his philosophical retinue, who already begin to mourn the passing of genius. All accept one. The haughty one, resplendent in red. Marcus clutches his arm, but he appears not to notice, or care. Commodus. The son, the wastrel, who will bring the great empire into such ill-repute. The chaos to come predicted in the cast of his feminine features. The curve of his sensuous mouth, the bleakness in his black, beady stare.

Chris looked back at Bradley. He thought he could see the same expression, hidden behind all that bad skin, in the face that regarded him from across the room.

Thunder crashed.

#

It had been a chance meeting in a local pub. Chris had recognised him from dust jackets and the net.

'Mr. Allsopp, sir…this is an honour…'

'Oh, please, call me Dominic, dear boy.'

Chris had known he lived in the general area but never thought he would ever meet him.

'This is such a, a…pleasure for me, sir, Mr – ah – D-D-Dominic, sir…I've read all of your books…ah…may I say, *The Perversions of Elagabalus*…a triumph!'

'Oh! Such praise! You know, I think I might grow to like you…'

Chris had relocated when the company had decided to consolidate. In the depressed economy he couldn't afford to refuse an offer. He wasn't happy, more used to an urban environment. He found open spaces confronting. From a family on the extreme end of working class, he'd only ever known bitumen and drab brick buildings, packed close.

Despite his situation, Chris had been a lover of history from an early age, though always aware that he would never be a candidate, via either genius or wealth, for classical education. But he had an eager mind, and the local library was adequate

118

enough, not to mention those few remaining second-hand bookshops.

'Dominic, I love the ancients. I adore our past... '

'Oh, dear boy, that is quite clear. You can't fake passion! And say, if you have such a drive for things hoary, you simply must come visit. I have an extensive library, which I suspect might be right up your alley. Not far from here, just follow the road north...top of the way?'

One visit had become two, become several. Dominic, always generous with his time, his books. He had a wealth that went back to before the first Great War. Retired from Cambridge, now a gentleman of leisure. A committed bachelor. His market farm, just a hobby, really. A chance to engage with the community.

'One does what one can to help our nation's youth...ah, that one! In that tight shirt...do you think she's being deliberately provocative? Here, let me freshen your glass...'

The library had elaborate French windows that opened out onto the back terrace. From where they usually sat, the enormous vegetable garden and the local teenagers who worked it could be seen. But Chris was always more drawn by the sumptuous interior. Numerous shelves of countless books, some dating back centuries! Cabinets of the most delicate – not to mention expensive – *objets d'art*, culled from some of the world's most prestigious auctions. The floorboards were polished, and scattered about were the finest Turkish rugs. The Adam style ceilings, simply breath-taking...

'Oh! Those two! That chubby one, and that guy with the crew cut...see them? Those are the ones I told you about. Found them only this morning, snogging behind the tool shed. Had his hand riiight up! Oh, mark my words, if that one's still innocent, well, she won't be for long...'

Chris would always blush, and give a little smile to such comments. He would stay quiet, let the moment pass. Didn't like their conversations becoming so earthy. He respected old

Dominic too much. Hell, he revered the man.

'And that one. Let me tell you…'

#

Tina returned with the Midori. She handed it to Kerri and crumpled back into the sofa.

Rain and wind continued to rattle the window.

Chris said, 'So, you say Dominic is out?'

'What ya think?' Bradley fired back.

'Huh?'

Bradley waited a beat.

'The paddock. The garden. We all put a lot of work in today. Looking good, yeah? Helped yourself, yeah?'

I have to get out of here. I have to!

He would try the front door. If Bradley chased him (and he felt certain he would) he could use his house keys, poked through his fingers. Hit him as hard as he could. Face, eyes…knee him in the balls maybe…

Maybe…

Chris tapped his left pocket, where the keys were. Then he tapped the right, unconsciously. He couldn't feel what was in there, but he knew it was. Why the hell did he put it there? An unconscious act? Possibly, but that didn't matter now. Right now it was the mistake that could finish him.

If he finds out…or does he already know?

'Um…w-well,' he tried, responding to the question, 'just thought I'd try a stew. H-had the peas already and…all the other stuff…just thought…Dominic said…'

'Oh, hey, sure. No probs. You're Dom's pal. It's all good.'

Bradley approached him. Chris felt his scrotum constrict.

Is this it?

#

It began as just a quick jaunt out on his bicycle, a breath of fresh air, a spot of exercise. Nothing drastic. But he had to start enjoying himself, had chosen the longer paths. Why not? His agoraphobia rapidly fading, given the welcome he'd received in his new home. Only light drizzle this morning. The locals offered promises of it clearing later. No reason to expect the clouds to gather, the heavens to open as they did.

A quick stop by Dominic's paddock. Grab a parsnip, maybe a carrot or two. Try something a bit more adventurous than a frozen meal tonight.

You're always welcome to help yourself. Anytime, my boy. You know that!

Chris didn't usually stop by on a Friday. Wednesdays were best for both. Or Thursdays sometimes, if impromptu meetings of the Caesar Society didn't interfere.

Chris should have trusted himself to make it home, but the rain had come so damn fast. He'd found the back door unlocked. He'd entered a dark passage, an unfamiliar place. He'd groped for lights. Found none. Feeling about, stumbling. He'd wanted to call out Dominic's name, but the silence had somehow shamed him. He shifted and struggled, somehow found himself in the hall that led to the living room.

He heard a noise. At the same time, his feet met an obstacle. He reached down and found a hessian sack that bulged. He fished out his mobile and thumbed the light on.

At first, he wasn't sure exactly what he was seeing. He fished about, found gilt boxes, objects of gold and silver. A candle stick, a tarnished figurine. He reached deeper – knives and folks stinging his fingers, a photo frame or a mirror? Down further – small, hard objects. He let the light play around. More sacks. He took a step back and his ankle grazed up against another bag.

He aimed the light and delved. He found soft cloth, stinging sequins. Reaching down, he found hard plastic. He dredged out a fistful of discs. DVDs, all secured in clear plastic cases. The discs were white, and all neatly labelled. He had to hold the phone closer.

RAPE OF THE SABINE WOMEN, the first label read. Chris knew his Livy, understood the reference. He thumbed the disc away.

TIBERIUS, AND HIS LITTLE FISHES, read the next. Chris felt a shiver. He knew his Suetonius and Tacitus as well, and tried to fathom the meaning. An idea brought acid to his gut. He thumbed.

THE HUMILIATION OF BOUDICA.

Thumbed.

THE FOURTH CRUSADE – A HARLOT UPON THE THRONE.

Thumbed.

LOT AND HIS DAUGHTERS – REFUGEES OF SODOM.

Thumbed.

SOCIETY OF THE INIMITABLE LIVERS.

Chris heard a sound. Footsteps and a scrape. He let the other discs fall, honestly didn't remember stuffing the last one into his pocket.

There was a fluttering, the sounds of creaks.

Chris felt the fear suddenly like a slap. It was obvious what was going on. He needed to escape. He moved down the hall, trying to retrace his steps, feeling suddenly disorientated. He thought of Dominic, fleetingly, but he was no help to him here. He needed to get out, escape…he needed the police…

More sounds up ahead.

He dashed back, past the sacks, into the kitchen. It was pitch-black. He worked by touch. He found the living room.

Where now?

Try the front door? Hide in the library?

Out the French windows, across the paddock…

He made for the library entrance, until he heard a sound that made him feel a cold blade in his bowels.

'Eeeee!' A high-pitched squeal.

122

He turned, and there was the blonde. The look on her face!

'Ahhhh....' Chris gurgled.

Then Kerri appeared. He had no idea from where. She looked less shocked. Guilty, rather.

'Ahhhh...h-h-hello!'

'Bradley,' Kerri said.

'I, um, I-I was just wondering...Dominic...'

'Brad! Come here now!'

#

Now, here they were.

Bradley continued to approach. Chris felt the urge to flee. By sheer force of will, he managed to stay exactly where he was. He tried to read Bradley's body language, marked the swagger. The little thug still wore the smirk, but his eyes were black and cold. Chris slipped his hand into his pocket, left it there when Bradley stopped, about a couple of metres away.

To the left was the way that led to the front door. Chris calculated his chances, felt a weakness in his knees. Kerri got up from the sofa. She'd neglected her Midori, left it on the side table. Even Tina shifted, untucked her feet and placed them on the floor.

'Now, listen,' Bradley said. His voice dropped in tone and he leaned forward.

Christ...what?

'Like, as I said, you and old Dom were good friends, yeah? Real pals? You love all that history stuff...and I'm wondering if you shared other interests?'

Bradley gave Chris a slow sly wink.

The hell?

'Tell me, Chris...which one d'you like best, huh? I'm guessing Kerri. Bit more up top...in more ways than one...'

Kerri took a few steps forward. She frowned.

'Brad?' she said.

123

'Of course,' Bradley continued, completely ignoring her, 'the blonde is a real goer…you can trust me on that…'

Chris spared a quick look. Now Tina was standing, wincing, her arms folded tightly across her chest.

'I noticed you, y'know?' he said. 'Noticed you both. Watching from the big window. You and Dom. Did you enjoy the view?'

'Brad?' Kerri tried again.

'Shut it!' He spat the words through a mouth that looked suddenly like it tasted something sour. He didn't look at Kerri, kept his eyes focused on Chris. As quick as his lips had changed, they reverted back to that wicked smirk.

Bradley licked his lips. 'C'mon, what do you say? This could be our little secret, yeah?'

'Brad?' Kerri said again, louder this time. 'What are you-'

'I said shut it, bitch!' There was now real venom in his voice. This time, he looked back over his shoulder, and both girls froze. 'Just shut your fucking whore mouth!'

Chris took a step back, came up against the glass cabinet beside the window. Things rattled. He spared a glance. Its height stood to the level of his chest. Littered with several delicate trinkets. On top sat a bronze bust, almost the size of a man's head. Chris' vision greyed around the edges. He tried to focus.

'It was you! You and that scrawny slut there,' Bradley continued. Chris barely listened. 'You two got us into this mess, and I'm the one trying to get us out. Now, keep your dirty rots shut, and let the men talk.'

The bust had cold handsome features. No expression. A dead empty stare.

Alexander! Chris thought, then, idiotically: *What would Alexander do?*

'But Brad, you can't-'

'Ah, fuck!' Bradley roared. He turned his back squarely on Chris, took steps towards Kerri, who backpedalled into the smaller girl behind her. Tina gave an audible sob.

'If I have to tell you again…'

Have to…Chris felt close to weeping.

'Now,' Bradley said. He started to turn back to face Chris. 'Where was – '

The bust was heavy. Chris had to lift it with both hands. He acted without thinking, letting instinct take over completely. One blind swing caught Bradley at the shoulder. He gave a breathy gasp and went to the floor. Kerri and Tina screamed at the same time, and Chris bolted.

It was dark, he was panicked, and he tripped, went to his knees, got up. The front door was just ahead, and it was wide open, but it was blocked by something he couldn't quite make out. He had to bruise against it, skin himself, to understand exactly what it was.

A van, the back doors wide open. It was backed up almost flush against the front door. For precious seconds, Chris thought he was trapped. He began to weep, pushing and pulling uselessly at the frame. Then he realised he could just squeeze his thin body around the side.

'Ah…you bastard!' Bradley's voiced was strained but sounded just too close. Chris edged himself around the van, ran blindly.

He was drenched within the first three steps. The rain was hammering down. It stole his vision, stole all other sound. Fear threatened to steal his sanity. He ran without plan or direction, found his stockinged feet sink into soft ground. It slowed him down, began to exhaust him quickly. He gulped for air. The ground began to rise, grew steeper. He used his hands. His heart was hammering like the rain, and his ribs ached. He kept expecting to feel Bradley's hand upon him at any instant.

Please Jesus…please God!

He continued to climb, until his limbs became lead and he could only wriggle and flounder. He made no more progress. He flipped over on his back. He was dead, anyway. He had to see. But the night and the storm continued to confound him. Only the few lights on in the house, and two twin lights lower down – the van? – gave him any frame of reference.

Done. I'm done.

He lay like one dead, letting the rain pound him into the ground. Only a matter of time before they found him. He tried to reflect and focus on the words of the Stoics. He tried to recall the sayings of Epictetus but had lost the words.

'I want to live!' he screamed into the mud. 'Please!'

For answer, he heard the faintest grumble. At first, he thought it was just more thunder. But he opened his eyes, looked to the house. Those lights were still on, but the lights of the van were gone from the front. Yes! Moving off from the long drive, onto the road, moving away.

Chris stayed down in the essential clay. He was still afraid. Was this a trap? He waited. Nothing happened. He waited. The van did not return. He waited. He was frozen. The ground sucked at him. The rain was destroying him.

He stirred, pushed himself to his feet. He needed shelter. He could try for home, ring the police from there. That was the safest option.

One almighty shiver shook his entire frame.

I'll die if I don't...

He walked back to the house. At first, he moved cautiously, almost crouching. The rain continued to fall hard.

The front door was wide open. He slinked back into the living room.

He was alone. He sneezed. He felt weak. Wincing, he moved to the downstairs bathroom, not caring about the mess he was making on the expensive shag pile. He peeled off his anorak, then his shirt and trousers, underpants and socks. He was so cold. There was a heater. He flicked it on. Clean, fluffy towels appeared; a godsend.

He lost himself to a fit of sneezing which almost sent him to his knees again. He rubbed himself vigorously, slapped at his

126

stinging muscles. The towels helped, but they weren't enough. He would need dry clothes.

He found the stairs. The dash up them hurt. He reached the second floor and slapped for the light switch, found it. Fear of Brad had given way to the hard possibility of pneumonia. He turned left on a whim, found the bedroom third door down. The fourth door was slightly ajar, and the light was on. He stopped, listened for sounds for a second, but his current needs couldn't be denied.

Dominic's bedroom was huge, exactly like Chris had imagined. It was dominated by a canopied bed with the most impressive gold-embossed bedspread. One corner had been turned down, but it was otherwise undisturbed, made perfectly. There were elaborate rugs and ornate furniture. He found the clothes in an adjoining room on the left. He wandered through them, lost in all the silks and finest cottons. He looked for the least elaborate attire, chose a snow-white shirt and grey woollen trousers. Dominic was a couple of inches shorter than Chris, but otherwise it was a relative easy match.

Instead of a jacket or jumper, he opted for a thick bathrobe he found hanging in the ensuite. The slippers were a rather tighter fit, but they warmed his feet almost immediately, so he didn't begrudge the minor discomfort.

There was a comfortable chair beside the bed. For several seconds, he sat with eyes closed, and just tried to process the recent events. His thoughts were jumbled. He wasn't good in a crisis. He fished for his mobile phone.

Ah! Downstairs.

He didn't want to get up. He wanted to sleep, didn't want the hectic interrogation that would come when the police arrived. He really craved a scotch now, just a splash over some ice. Maybe take it to the library. That place always made him feel at home.

Yes...

But then he launched himself out of the chair. He cursed

himself for a weakling and a poor friend. He had assumed that Dominic was dead, but what if he was only injured, in pain, suffering somewhere? And was he really going to waste time, let those wretched delinquents get away with…

He stalked from the room. His first thought was to retrieve his phone, still in his sodden anorak. He walked with purpose, had made the top of the stairs, then he stopped and looked back.

The fourth room, with the light that was on.

Perhaps…

He took a deep breath and retraced his steps. He was tense and walked slowly. He didn't want to go there, so he waited a moment to compose himself.

He nudged the door.

Another big room, illuminated by well-positioned lamps. The type found in film and television production. They were switched on and were all aimed at the centre of the room, where a raised platform supported three padded benches and some low tables, scattered with grapes and other ripe fruit, as well as spilled goblets of wine. The furniture was low, the legs bowed and shapely. Finely woven fabrics and bright cushions gave the suggestion of elegant comfort. Beyond the platform was a backdrop, floor to ceiling, depicting naked dancers, and, off to the sides, couples reclining in amorous embraces as they either watched on, or looked to their own entertainments.

'My God.'

It was a set. A depiction of a dining scene from ancient Rome. Chris looked over his shoulder. The lamps were blinding but he still noticed a tripod, yet no camera. He approached the platform – or perhaps dais was a better term – walked up onto it. He picked up a cushion. His skin tingled at the velvet texture. He examined the backdrop more closely. Yes, he had seen it before, in books. Photos of the frescoes that still existed from lost Herculaneum. He looked down at a halved pomegranate. The juice, rich as blood, stained one of the tables. It dripped down, and a surprisingly long trail continued on to the back of the dais.

And that's where he saw him.

'Oh!'

Dominic was dressed in a purple toga. His face was pale but his cheeks were pink with bogus vitality. Make-up, same as the deep green eyelids and scarlet lips. He was on his back, one hand on his chest, the other flung off to the side.

Chris kneeled on the dais and leaned over. He held his hand above Dominic's mouth but felt nothing. After a brief hesitation, he touched his neck, again, nothing.

'Dominic.'

He could see no damage to the corpse, no signs of violence. The toga was hitched up close to around his hips, showing off his spindly legs. The toenails that poked out of his red dyed sandals were sparkling silver.

Chris looked away, feeling ill. He got back to his feet and left the room. He made his way downstairs, back to the bathroom, and took his keys and phone from the anorak.

Now to call for the police, and probably an ambulance too, as pointless as that would be. He worked the screen with his forefinger, swiped up the dial pad.

He stopped.

He stood, considering. He crouched down and pulled the DVD out of his other pocket. He read the label again.

SOCIETY OF THE INIMITABLE LIVERS.

He couldn't help but consider.

Oh, no. Don't do it. Don't you dare.

Dominic had a player and a small plasma screen in his library, concealed away so as not to interfere with the décor. Chris knew where it was hidden.

But you can't play it. You don't want to see it.

Chris put the phone in the pocket of the dressing gown. He walked back into the living room, then over to the library.

You won't forgive yourself.

The light was already on. He made his way through the

129

shelves, came to the painting of Pasiphae and the Bull of Minos. He took it down. He turned on the DVD player, fed in the disc.

No!

He aimed the remote, pressed the on button with his thumb. He stood unmoving, looking at the blank screen. It needed seconds to warm up. He thought fast, finally decided he needed that drink now. He left the library, poured himself a generous three fingers, and took a sip.

He thought about the Ptolemies, the last great Dynasty of Egypt. Cleopatra, the last of that degenerate, inbred line. The ancient writers had derided her decadent lifestyle. The Romans had condemned her as a foreign whore.

The Inimitable Livers.

The drinking society she'd founded with Marc Antony. Plutarch had written of wild extravagance, the vulgar display of wealth and power. Over time, it had become a fantasy, an excuse to imagine the vilest orgies. Indeed, it was one of Dominic's favourite topics...'Dear boy! Imagine the lengths that worthy doxie might have gone to! The depths she might have plumbed!'

Chris finished his drink. His hand trembled.

Kerri. She might just be old enough.

But Tina?

He lingered at the drinks tray. He was a study of indecision. He knew that, no matter what he finally decided, he would hate himself.

He put the empty glass down and walked back to the library. He walked with determination, turned the corner, and saw the screen. He froze, going cold all over.

The DVD was playing.

Oh, Christ.

He saw two figures but was too far away to make them out clearly. He approached the television, snatched up the remote. Now that he was closer, he could see a lot clearer.

It was Kerri and Brad. They were upon the dais. She was

reclining on a divan, holding a goblet. He was standing, adopting a dramatic stance; arms raised, legs akimbo. It looked absolutely ridiculous. But even that was trumped by his costume consisting of a plastic breastplate and short tunic that didn't reach his surprisingly knobbly knees. He wore greasy make-up, inches thick, and a wig of tight curls that shone beneath the lights. He was talking, and the volume was on, but Chris could barely hear him. This was certainly not a professional production. The camera microphone was too far away, just barely catching anything they said. He heard Dominic's prompts, though, coming from behind the camera. Though no enthusiast of Shakespeare, Chris suspected they were the words of the Immortal Bard.

He quickly turned his attention to Kerri. She was Cleopatra, of course. Again, the costume was complete tat; square-cut dark wig, diadem in the shape of an asp, faux silver sandals. But it was her abundant cleavage, provided by the artful folding of her purple robe, which was her most distinguished feature. Indeed, as if reading Chris' mind, the camera jiggled slightly, then moved jerkily closer, until Kerri's chest filled the shot. It lingered there for several seconds, took in a close-up her heavily made up face (kohl-rimmed eyes and jade lips, applied liberally) and trailed back along her body as it moved back to its original position.

The scene dragged on. The two exchanged halting, gaff-ridden dialogue, constantly corrected by Dominic's commanding voice. Chris raised the remote, about to jump ahead, when suddenly Brad exclaimed:

'Some wine here! And our vi-vi-violins! Fortune knows we scorn her most when she blows us!'

At the call, Tina entered the scene. Chris blushed, but he didn't look away. The blonde carried a tray laden with fruit and a jug. She wore the scantiest harness of leather and silk that barely clothed her nudity, instead strangely enhancing it. Her skin was stained a desolate saffron, her lips the colour of saviour's blood. She minced timidly into the scene. Bradley grabbed the jug of wine, quaffed it. He grabbed her up in his other brawny arm. The tray clattered, apples and plumbs scattering.

Bradley began to cover Tina's small breasts with savage kisses. He threw her down hard upon the other divan, began dry humping her as she worked at the linen that girded his loins. Kerri watched with hungry interest.

Chris felt dizzy. He glanced away. There was, on a lower shelf, a six-volume leather-bound set of Gibbon's *Decline and Fall*. A couple of shelves above, he saw *Petronius and Juvenal*, *Martial and Apuleius*. On a sudden vicious whim, he clawed at them and let them fall to the floor. He turned about, found a commentary on the fragments of *Zeno*. He clutched it to his chest. He stood with his back to the screen, telling himself he couldn't hear the grunting, nor the heavy sighs. He recalled the words of Epictetus, Seneca, tried to conjure with them, tried to maintain calm.

He turned back to face the screen. This time he would turn it off. But his hand didn't move to the remote. He froze, felt a terrible chill in his belly.

'God...'

Dominic had entered the scene, the camera now fixed in a wide shot. He had taken Tina away from Bradley, had her down on the floor, on her hands and knees. Brad and Kerri were coupling in a frenzied manner upon a divan.

'Dominic...oh, hell...'

The older man was just about naked, the white costume he must have been wearing already thrown aside. Only a few slender gold chains offered a sop to modesty. His flaccid body was stained a jet black, like soot, and where he handled the blonde, it stained her as well. One hand was gripping her shoulder, the other pressing down on her back. If he was generous, Chris might have said she looked uncomfortable, but really what he read was pain and humiliation in that slack jaw and those haunted eyes.

Dominic's wig was big and woolly. Massively so, ludicrous. No doubt his idea of a joke. No denying his imperialistic streak, all those quips about 'wogs' and 'fuzzy-wuzzies'. Chris couldn't have been more shocked if he'd seen the old man with a bone threw his nose. Probably portraying himself an emissary from the Sudan, no doubt he couldn't resist a bit of racist caricature.

His eyes were rolled back into his head. His chest heaved. He was pushing himself, and Tina, hard.

Chris felt his guts boiling. He couldn't watch any more. He left the scene playing, turned and walked away. Out of the library, out of the house. He left the front door hanging open. The rain still fell, but not nearly with as much fury as before. It was still dark, and he stumbled many times, but his inner radar worked, surprisingly, and he made it home, muddied, slightly bruised, but otherwise no worse for wear. He let himself in the through back door and found his way through the kitchen, down the hall, to his favourite chair, near his bookshelves in his own modest library. He fumbled and found the lamp. He squinted, trying to focus. He still had the copy of *Zeno,* a gilt embossed hardcover. He opened it and found the rain had made the pages sodden and mashed. Unreadable.

He wept.

#

Bradley's only plan was to head north, so it was not really a plan at all. He had no friends up there, no contacts of any kind. No idea what he might expect, only that 'up north' offered contrast, a foreign place far away. So that is where they were headed.

The van belonged to his brother. He'd let him borrow it for the night under the condition that Brad would return it with a full tank and not a scratch. Eddy had gone to the local with his mates, so when they left Dom's place, Brad had taken a chance, stopped by home just quick enough to swipe Ed's secret stash of money and coke that he must have thought he'd hidden so carefully in the loft. If he'd been caught, a beating was the least he could have expected. But he'd got clear away, and there was no way he was ever going back home again.

He'd been driving for hours and he still felt wide awake. The coke helped, of course, but also the urgent need to put as much distance between them and that dead old fuck as he could. No doubt that tosser, Chris, had called the cops as soon as they'd left. Soon enough, they would have to find a place to hole up for a while…but not just yet…just a few more miles…

The girls were in the back. He'd ordered them there. All those whiney bloody questions! They'd got on his nerves, so he'd packed them out of harm's way.

'Go on, Kerri. Best thing. You're really getting on my wick, and you don't want me to kick you off, do you?' he'd said.

That left him alone to consider his options. They'd managed to gather quite a haul before making their dash, quite a bit of gold and silver, but they hadn't found any cash. The old bastard no doubt had a hidden safe somewhere. They did have his brother's money, but that would only get them so far. Soon enough he'd have to make contacts, find a fence, convert what they'd stolen for hard currency. Then what? Leave the country? They'd need plenty of cash for that. New clothes, fake passports, flights…

'Awww, shit!'

Brad slapped the steering wheel. Who the fuck was he kidding? No chance of that. And no matter where they went within the country, no matter where they tried to hole up, in even the most out of the way place, the police would be hunting them, every step.

His vision blurred. He blinked rapidly. He rubbed at his neck and his shoulder. It still frigging hurt like a son of a bitch where that arsehole had hit him.

If I could have found the prick...

Yes, well? What would he have done? How far would he have gone? The fact was, he wasn't nearly as hard as the outward façade he presented to the world. The cops must already suspect of him of foul play at the very least, probably of manslaughter. Perhaps even...

'Fuck!'

It had been a simple plan to start with. A spur of the moment decision, after the ancient bastard had keeled over, right in the process of taking Tina doggy-style on the floor. He always had liked Tina best, and he always pushed himself too hard, no matter how many times they'd warned him to take it easy. One second, bashing away, drool on his lips, that feral look in his eye. The next, stone-cold dead.

Kerri and Tina had just wanted to cut and run. But Brad was a forward thinker. They'd had a very good thing going with old Dom; he'd paid well for their services, and now that he'd carked it, that well had dried up. They needed something to tide them over, and anyway, they deserved a severance package of some kind. The old perve owed them, dammit!

So just take a few things, stash them somewhere. People knew they visited Dom often, but they always arranged alibis for when he asked them to one of his filming sessions. Hell, no one could have proven they were there.

Until that bastard Chris had shown up.

Fucker! Ruined us!

And, when the uptight wanker wouldn't go along with the deal he had for him, Brad had panicked. No time, he reasoned, to put all the gear back before the old bill arrived; not enough courage (he admitted, but only to himself) to silence Chris in any permanent way...the girls were underage, they'd pull through, but he was now too old for remand...

His driving became erratic as he considered his meagre options. He tried to tell himself to calm down. Luckily, there was no one else about on the back roads at that time of the morning. At the last place they'd stopped to fill up, Brad had also bought a couple of tins of kerosene, and a shovel. He still had to get rid of all those DVDs and photos, and he didn't know whether to burn them or bury them? Or maybe head for the coast, throw them off some pier?

The nerves were eating him again. Another line or two of coke, that's what he needed. It was a long, dark stretch of road. Good a place as any. He slowed the van, pulled over.

It was cold, but at least there was no more rain. Brad paced about, pin-wheeling his arms and stamping his feet. He patted the pocket of his jeans, where he kept the coke. He'd already taken quite a few hits in the last few hours.

'Just two lines more,' he promised himself.

First, he walked around to the front of the van, unzipped and got his cock out. The thick stream of piss he let loose didn't solve all of his problems, but helped relieve the stress a little.

He was just about finished when he sensed movement behind him. He tensed, then he heard Kerri speak. Her voice was timid.

'Brad? Why have we stopped? Everything okay?'

'Uh huh,' he grunted. 'If you need to piss, do it now. We still have some driving to do.'

He turned to face her. She wore the Cleopatra wig and the purple robe, cinched at her waist with a thick, ornate belt. It accentuated her figure. Her face was thick with make-up, made her look more mature. Black eye shadow and gold, pouting lips.

'What the fuck is this?'

She tried a smile. 'H-How do I look?'

'Why the hell did you bring that shit? I said only stuff we could sell! All that crap is useless to us.'

'Awww…just a few little things. We didn't think you'd mind. And we brought a few things for you too.'

She reached down and picked up the plastic breast plate. She offered it and, nonplussed, Brad took it out of her hands.

'And here, this also.' She held up a gold circlet, shaped to

136

look like entwined laurel leaves. The one Dom had worn when he played Emperor. The very one he'd been wearing when he died.

'You were always our conqueror,' she said, 'never old Dom.'

Bradley looked her up and down.

'There's no one around. Maybe we could stop here a bit? You need a break.'

'Get back in the van,' he said. 'Wait there. I'll be around in a second.'

Kerri smiled. Without another word she skipped out of his sight, back to where Tina was waiting, looking fretful. She wore an elaborate headdress and had rouged cheeks and heavy jewellery around her thin wrists and ankles. Little else. Kerri climbed in and gave her a hug.

'Don't worry. It will all be all right.'

They waited, holding each other, not talking. A minute or so later, Bradley appeared. Eyes wide, the cruel sneer on his lips. He wore the breastplate and laurel. He worked at his belt as he climbed into the van.

'Mine honour was not yielded, but conquered merely,' Kerri said.

'Veni vidi vici,' Bradley replied. His pitch was perfect.

Author Biographies

Danielle Birch loves to write about tormented souls who have lost their path in life. Her short stories have been published in various anthologies and magazines, including *Lighthouses: An Anthology of Dark Tales*, and she is currently working on her first novel. She is a coffee (and wine) enthusiast and novice gardener who lives in a house filled with books in bayside Brisbane, Australia, with her husband and Kelpie. www.daniellebirch.com

Claire Fitzpatrick is an author and poet of speculative fiction and non-fiction. She has been a panellist at Conflux in Canberra and Continuum in Melbourne. Her non-fiction has been nominated for Shadows and Aurealis Awards. Called 'Australia's body horror specialist' by Bartholomew Ford from Breach Magazine, she enjoys writing about the human body and the dark side of humanity. She lives in Brisbane. Visit her at www.clairefitzpatrick.net

Cameron Trost is a writer of strange, mysterious, and creepy tales about people just like you. He is the author of *Hoffman's Creeper and Other Disturbing Tales* and *The Tunnel Runner,* and is the creator of *Oscar Tremont, Investigator of the Strange and Inexplicable*. He hails from Australia but now lives in France, between the rugged coast of Brittany and the vineyards of the Loire. Castles, forests, storms, and whisky are a few of his favourite things. www.camerontrost.com

Stuart Olver is an enthusiastic reader of horror and science fiction, and sometimes manages to put a few words together as well. He has been published in Writing Queensland, Howard Horror, Midnight Echo, and also in several anthologies. Born in Durban, South Africa, he now lives in Brisbane, Australia with his wife and two sons, and is happiest when pottering around snow-capped mountains.

Jeremy Hayes lives in Ontario, Canada, where he enjoys writing fantasy novels and strange short stories. He is the author of *The Goblin Squad*, a children's fantasy novel, along with *The Stonewood Trilogy* and its spinoff book, *Evonne and Vrawg: Bounty Hunters*. He has a particular interest in weird fiction and released a collection of short stories entitled *Tales Most Strange*, with the follow-up, Even More Tales Most Strange, coming soon. www.northlordpublishing.com

Pym Schaare is an author who explores the dynamics of the ordinary in her characters when they are facing extraordinary situations. She seeks to show the interplay between her characters' internal and external worlds and how that frames the way they behave in the context of the plot. Born in Berlin, Pym migrated to Australia with her parents in the sixties, and now calls the leafy, sultry suburb of Highgate Hill in Brisbane home. She has written feature articles, essays, short stories, poetry, and a novel. *Since Then: Poems and Commentary* is available from Wheelers.

Mark McAuliffe lives in Brisbane. Since the 1990s, he has had stories and poetry appear in several small press publications. Most recently, he has been published in the anthologies, *An Eclectic Slice of Life, In Sunshine Bright and Darkness Deep*, and *Lighthouses: An Anthology of Dark Tales*.

Also Available from Black Beacon Books

The Black Beacon Book of Horror features dark and disturbing tales from some of the most original and imaginative authors writing in the genre today.

www.ingramcontent.com/pod-product-compliance
Lightning Source LLC
Chambersburg PA
CBHW030536130626
46552CB00006B/2278